Obliquity

STORIES OF A TILTED PERSPECTIVE

First printing, 2016
Second printing, 2017

0 1 2 3 4 5 6 7 8 9

Paperback ISBN: 978-0-9944614-7-6
Digital ISBN: 978-0-9925201-9-9

1231 Publishing
PO Box 77
Kallangur QLD 4503
Australia

OBLIQUITY

noun

1. deviation from moral rectitude or sound thinking

2. a: deviation from parallelism or perpendicularity; also : the amount of such deviation

   b : the angle between the planes of the earth's equator and orbit having a value of about 23°27' <obliquity of the ecliptic>

3. a : indirectness or deliberate obscurity of speech or conduct
conduct

   b : an obscure or confusing statement

definition referenced from
Merriam-Webster dictionary

CONTENTS

CONTENTS

UNDERCURRENT

Linda Conlon

The sunset was a spectacular blaze; a pugilist's palette of bruised purples, bright pinks, swollen reds and golds so livid as to appear green. They lit up the world beyond the panel of windows Annalise was facing. Reclining tentatively on a plush lounge, she felt aligned with the sky. Tender. Battered. Broken.

Doctor Adam glanced up from his session notes and noticed her enraptured expression. Swivelling to see what she was looking at, he realised he hadn't brought the shades down. One click later, the room descended into a darkness punctured by mellow lamps at either end of her couch and another on the table by the psychologist's elbow.

"How has your week been?" he queried in his rich bass.

Annalise swallowed as she regarded him. He looked like any other bearded hipster but he wielded a surprising weapon; the vocal stylings befitting a god. If melted chocolate could speak, it would sound like Corey Adam, D. Psych. The question—deliciously delivered though it might be—was banal but it stirred a brittle sensation between her vertebrae. She wasn't ready for confrontation but suspected she was about to be emotionally flayed and exposed to her core. She wasn't sure how to become okay with that.

"Alright."

There was a pause that indicated he'd expected more from her. "Have you spoken to your sister?"

Annalise licked her lips, wanting to be diplomatic despite the tautness overcoming her face. "Of course, a few times. Nothing enlightening, just wedding stuff. She's pressuring me to get the hen's night organised."

Doctor Adam smiled, his gaze sliding over her countenance, picking up all her unspoken tells like aphids feeding on a rose. "As is the maid of honour's duty, I understand," he murmured sympathetically.

Annalise snorted quietly, concentrating on loosening the fists clenched upon her stomach. "Yes, though I don't know why she bothered calling me that. She's going to organise it all and have everything exactly the way she wants it anyway. I'm just the idiot that has to make the phone calls. I have six *months*, but the way she acts, it's like I have six *days* to get it all done," she complained, exasperation seeping through.

It wasn't enough that the whole reason she was even *in* therapy was because of Briony and Garth's ridiculous beach wedding. No, her little sister had to make it worse by harassing her regularly over the million other details Annalise was expected to get right. God forbid she take some time to get rid of her thalassophobia so that she could stand beside the overwhelming vastness of a fathomless ocean without crumpling into a screaming pile of tears and vomit—and endure the wedding.

Briony had made it painfully clear that Annalise was a terrible inconvenience and a malevolent blight bearing the potential of ruining the future Mr and Mrs Ryan's BIG DAY (how dare she?). As they'd grown up, Briony had tolerated Annalise's 'weird fear' because it hadn't impacted her blessed life. Now, if it was all the same to Annalise, Briony would prefer she just got *over* her fear of the ocean.

"And you're making excellent progress," Doctor Adam commended, drawing Annalise's thoughts away from spiteful imaginings and back to the present. "So let's continue. Tonight, we'll talk about the man we discovered during your last session—"

Annalise stiffened, heartrate thundering in her ears, making Doctor Adam's words inaudible.

No. Not again. He's private. I don't want to talk about him.

The words clogged her throat and she lay there in abject horror, trying to steady herself. It was as bad as she'd anticipated it might be, and this was only the first slice. She wanted to sit up but she also didn't want to show her hand. Like a dog, Doctor Adam could scent her terror and hone in on it with an obscene level of excitement. If she stayed calm, he might be persuaded out of thinking it was a big deal... though it was, of course.

In fact, there *was* no bigger deal. There was thalassophobia and him and sometimes it felt like those were the only parts that constituted her whole; not her family, not her job, not her friends or the books she liked to read nor the TV shows she watched.

She was defined by fear and *him*.

He'd always been there, in her dreams. His face was as familiar to her as her own, in all its forms— he'd grown as she had, maturing alongside her, like a childhood friend. He was more than that, though. And yet less. Ephemeral as a whisper but as abiding as memory, he was an echo in her bones and stamped in her blood. Where he ended and she began she'd never been able to tell, yet he was always an individual entity. He was just *hers*.

"I don't think he's anything to do with this," she blurted out, cutting the psychologist off.

He blinked at her, his next words trapped in his puffed-out cheeks until he released them with a soft pop. "What makes you say that?"

Annalise did sit up then, rubbing her fingers over the roughened skin at the back of her other hand. She licked her lips, forcing herself to make eye contact as she shrugged one shoulder with an affectation she hoped was at once convincingly casual while also insinuating dismissal of the subject.

The doctor was not to be so easily deterred. "What was it you said you called him?"

"Tim," she answered softly, wrapping her arms around her middle and lowering her gaze. The heat in her cheeks was palpable. It was silly, really, but having him so frequently in her head had spurred her to name him. As a child, she'd thought of him merely as 'the boy'. When they were both older that seemed immature, so she'd dubbed him 'The Man', shortened it to T.M. and it had progressed naturally to Tim.

"Right, well this Tim seems to be an integral part of your psyche, with credible influence over and integration into your memories. I know we didn't find any crossover *yet*, but it's entirely possible he's behind your thalassophobia." Doctor Adam paused, giving her a steady look. "I think he's the key to unlocking you."

It felt like everything inside her dropped out and she was a husk, sitting there reluctantly nodding, unable to raise any more objections. Doctor Adam was right; she knew it as surely as she knew her own name. She was deathly afraid he wouldn't be skilled enough to disentangle Tim from the fear and she'd lose them both.

"Please. Lie back," the doctor invited and she did as she was told, a cocoon of numbness engulfing her even while his words lulled her into a serene state of trust. Being hypnotised got easier every session and she was soon floating in reassuring sanctuary, a place where he promised nothing would harm her—so long as she maintained her focus on his voice.

"I will," she promised, compelled to speak because... she needed to forgive him? The oddness of the urge was an acrid lining in her throat but it faded as he continued.

"I want you to think about Tim," Doctor Adam instructed.

Warmth reverberated from his voice and through Annalise's body. She wanted to fight him but she was instantly out in a field of some sort, watching Tim dig with a hand hoe. She felt the burn of blisters inside gloved hands, the bite of sun on a bare back and smelled the soil. She knew its dryness came from being bled of its nutrients by overplanting. She felt worried for him and also knew that his emotions were seeping in to taint hers.

The scene changed, as did the season, and she was somewhere snowy. She blinked against a flurry of falling snowflakes and sun glinting off a frozen lake. A fence of some sort was in front of him but nestled in the lee of his arms was a woman. She was delicate and short but Annalise knew he loved her because she was softness and beauty coating a core of steel and determination. The need to marry her, to belong to her and be known as this woman's husband was everything thrumming in Tim's blood at that moment.

More snatches and flashes came; more even than Annalise had experienced in her dreams. She saw Tim on his wedding day, saw him shed tears of joy over a squalling baby, saw him commit those same manifestations of his soul to soil she knew was barren and unwilling to provide what his family so desperately needed. Each moment was prompted by Doctor Adam's distant voice but she was too intent on her connection to Tim to be fully aware of him.

Without warning, there came a dissonance. Tim was going to a beach—not like the ones Annalise knew, but one with smooth pebbles and grit rather than sand, and waves that churned and ran like grabbing hands over it all.

Annalise was frozen with terror.

Tim was nervous but excited.

There was a jetty and a boat hired and someone

rowing. With every stroke, Annalise shook harder, her stomach rebelling at her nearness to an ocean, even in her mind. Normally, she was unable to stand looking at pictures of an ocean. An image of someone diving in deep, dark water had stolen more than one night's sleep from her. This was torture. To Annalise, the ocean was a vast, gaping wound in the planet's crust, an earthen maw filled with deadly saltwater and nightmares. Tim looked at the roiling black clouds above and the restless ocean below and was not concerned.

Doctor Adam's voice was able to unclench her jaw enough for her to respond to his questions but she had difficulty explaining what she was seeing. The lure of the sanctuary was strong but the psychologist pressed her to stay in that sea-ravaged boat a little longer, to see what would happen. The winds picked up, the sky darkened and the water around the small vessel became choppy. Annalise *knew* Tim had to get off, get out, go home, but she couldn't make him. Try as she might, she'd never been able to direct him in any of her dreams, she could only ever watch.

An extra large wave struck nearby, creating a trench the small boat slid into and Tim toppled overboard into the ocean. Frozen in the moment, even Annalise was struck by its lack of drama and preamble. He was there and then he was... gone.

He can't swim, he's a farm boy, he's never been in the ocean in his life. He'll drown!

She was him and he was her in a way that had never happened. They tried to fight, to scoop the water beneath them and swim their way to the surface but when they got there, the boat had moved impossibly far away and the hands that reached to help were useless. A wave struck them on the right side of the head, filling their ear and distorting the chaotic noise of the storm. Another wave came and still another, dominating them and plunging them underwater, usurping their strength and slowing their frenzied clawing for the surface. Fear was suffocating them as they thrashed, air fading, lungs screaming, ever sinking into that treacherous wound. Arms flailed with less vigour and kicking legs became weights even though hearts beat with such thunder that it seemed nothing earthly could ever make them stop but the light... began to fade... and everything blackened and there was wickedness sheathed in that velvet darkness. A siren call of promised peace after only a moment's pain. Water gushed in, searing its way into lungs, jolting the one body left suspended in a salted cradle. The insidious sea was pleased by the life it claimed, its victory swift and absolute.

Annalise became aware of herself quite suddenly. She was sitting up, her cheeks cooled by evaporating tears, her nose running and her throat raw from screaming... or drowning. Doctor Adam perched on his seat, staring at her with an inscrutable expression that melted into triumph when he saw that she was properly awake.

"We found it," he told her softly, his deep voice vibrating with the voluptuous joy of solving an untenable problem. "That was your trigger."

"But... I've never seen that before," she answered unsteadily. Overall, her emotions were a kaleidoscope, fed by chills that clenched her spine.

Doctor Adam frowned. "What do you mean?"

"I mean I didn't know he drowned. I've never dreamed that before so how could *that* be my trigger? How can I have been scared my entire life by something that never happened to me and that I've never fucking seen before?!" she demanded, her voice suddenly shrill and angry. Anger was the easiest to latch onto.

The psychologist looked alarmed by her language but he wasn't swayed by her argument. "It might represent an event we haven't uncovered—"

"I've *asked*! You know I did. Mum, Dad, my grandparents, my aunts, uncles, cousins and just about the bloody lawnmower man all said the same thing—nothing with the ocean ever happened to me or anyone I knew as a child, I was just *born* fearing it!"

He frowned thoughtfully, saying nothing as he processed her outburst. She thought it was because she'd offended him but realised it wasn't when he next spoke.

"Do you know what an endoparasite is?"

"A what?"

"It's a parasite that lives inside the body or cells of a host."

"So?"

"I have a theory about Tim and why you're experiencing new things each time you dream about him or I put you under."

"That he's a parasite?" she asked incredulously, her head throbbing and her shoulders aching from hunkering against the storm.

"A *soul* parasite. An echo. A being that experienced a trauma so profound in his own life that he was compelled to perpetuate his existence by leeching from another, essentially finding life again. In you."

Annalise squinted and blinked, visualising the workings of her own mind like some weird sliding puzzle where the tiles were blocks of crumbling cheese. "You think..."

"... that Tim was an actual person. Once," Doctor Adam nodded. "And he followed you into this life, bequeathing you his demons. Until tonight, when you broke free of your shackles."

"That's... insane," she floundered.

His face developed a hardness of superiority she hadn't seen since their first session together when he'd extolled the virtues of his practice. "There are documented cases of this sort of thing happening, and your story matches those exactly. You've moved from having an inexplicable phobia and the presence of a life-long kindred to beginning to heal. It's a solid explanation. Doesn't that make you feel better?"

"Better?" she repeated hoarsely, finding the concept as foreign as another language.

Drowning with Tim had left her weak. She couldn't see how living without him would make her feel anything but empty and she didn't recall even *asking* for a 'solid explanation'. What would that change?

From the inside cover of his notes folio, Doctor Adam withdrew an image of an iceberg floating in a dark and mysterious ocean. He stabbed it towards her and she was compelled to look. For the first time, it didn't make her blanch and she was horrified by feeling only a minor quiver of apprehension. She didn't say anything but from the look on the psychologist's face, she didn't need to. He knew. His theory was right.

Annalise hated him passionately for it.

She gathered her things and left the office saying very little, his excited babbling about the breakthrough and their next session unperturbed by her silence. The numbness was back, stifling the awful sensation of abandonment that had come to impersonate her insides. It insulated her while she found her car and drove away from the scene of the crime, eager to hide inside her flat. She wanted to cry but couldn't. She wanted to scream but couldn't. She wanted to tell Doctor Adam he was wrong... but she couldn't.

Without being entirely certain of how she'd got all the way home and through the locked front door, she found herself in her bathroom, staring at her own reflection in an effort to convince herself of everything that she suddenly knew.

Tim died.

Her life had once been his. Doctor Adam said they'd shared a soul. But now she was alone. Her psyche had managed to swim out of those depths, while he drifted away.

He'd left her. She'd expelled him.

She'd never again see him in her dreams, or know the unique joy of being entwined with another. Yes, she was 'getting better'... but it felt like someone had taken a razor blade to every one of her cells and sliced it in half. She was raw. Bleeding. Bereft.

She grieved the part of herself she'd just watched die and hated herself for pursuing this awful idea. She was to blame for his loss. She'd felt something incongruous at the start of the session yet she hadn't got up and walked out. She couldn't deflect or defend this decision.

It was all her fault.

Perhaps she'd been violated by a fear and righteous thirst for life that wasn't hers but she'd never questioned it. She'd *enjoyed* bearing the remnants of his rage because Tim had also been a fascination and a comfort. She'd never felt crippled by a shadow that had eclipsed her; how could she? She'd never known it existed and having it postulated that she should enjoy being free to cast her *own* shadow now only left her despairing and infuriated.

She'd carried the secret of him around with her for her whole life, nurturing and protecting him, and it had never occurred to her — until it was far too late — that there would come an excision. An exorcism. That one day they'd be wrenched apart irrevocably and she'd be the reason.

Because her beginning could only be born upon his ending.

A LOVE NOTE
BY A DIFFERENT NAME

Sophie L. Macdonald

"Do you love me?" I whispered, not for the first time, laying my head on his shoulder and snuggling into his neck. The silence made me pull back and look up at him. I'd asked the question in a silly voice — a baby kind of voice — so that he would know I didn't mean it. I didn't really need him to tell me.

His eyes were focused somewhere far away and then he gave a little jump. "Of course, I do." He kissed me on the top of the head, the way you might kiss a child. "You know that."

"I do." I tilted my face up at him and he gave me a peck on the lips. So far removed from our first kiss: he'd stepped back and I stumbled.

"So, what do you want to do today?" he asked brightly.

I hesitated. "I don't know." I was thrown. I thought he would have planned something.

"Well, today is in your hands," he announced grandly. "It's your day after all."

"Our day," I said.

"Yes, our day." His smile faded and he squeezed the tops of my arms. "You know what I mean. I want it to be special for you. Whatever you feel like doing."

"I want it to be special for both of us," I said, trying for a smile. "Do you remember our first Valentine's Day together?"

So many years ago now. It was a Saturday, and he had let me sleep in. I'd woken at ten and stumbled downstairs to find that he had laid up the kitchen table with croissants, ham, pain au chocolat, and the cheese that I like with the holes. In the fridge were two glasses of Bucks Fizz, already poured. He had sat there at the table—I have no idea how long for—looking as if he had been expecting me that precise second. He could have been there for hours. He'd planned a beautiful day where we walked by the river, had a late picnic on the bank, and then dinner at a tiny Japanese restaurant near home. He hated Japanese food but knew that I loved it. It was an amazing day.

"Yes, I remember," he smiled. "Never been able to look sushi in the eye since."

I laughed but it was a short laugh. "That was the best breakfast I ever had." We both glanced at the kitchen table, where my cereal bowl was still sitting. I picked it up and put it in the dishwasher. Luke had already cleared his toast plate away. I'd been in the shower whilst he'd eaten this morning.

"So, you want to go for a picnic, is that it?" He glanced out of the window. "It's a bit overcast today. Could be chilly."

"No, it doesn't have to be a picnic." I shrugged. "What do you fancy?"

"There are a few things I'd like to do," he said. "Just some jobs I've been meaning to do in the garden. How about I get those done and then we go for dinner later?"

"Sure," I said.

"But no raw fish this time!" he laughed.

"No."

"Well, I should get started." He patted me on the shoulder. "How about you organise somewhere for dinner?" I nodded and watched him leave.

When I was a child I was horrified at my parents' lack of romance. My mum used to find it funny. "Things change when you've been married a while, Rach," she would say. "You still love each other, but it's different. You're more comfortable with each other. You're not trying to impress the other person all the time. You're more secure. It's a deeper love."

"But I want love I can feel," I would say.

"Oh, you can still feel it," she'd answer. "You just have to look beyond the surface."

I went to the window and watched Luke start up the mower. He always did the outside work as he knew I hated it. I caught his eye and he waved. I waved back and started to clear up the kitchen. My cup of tea was still warm. He made me a cup of tea every morning before we left for work. Sometimes we didn't even see each other, as we were too busy flying in different directions to get out of the door, but my cup of tea was always there on the counter like a love note. I'm thinking of you. I love you. Have a good day.

I smiled and cradled the warm cup between my hands. Valentine's Day gets better with time. You just have to look beyond the surface.

DESTINATION: ME

R. A. Purtill

I will never know why I answered the call of his thumb.

Compassion? Desperation? The lure of unexpected adventure, perhaps? But as I pulled over and invited him into my precious yellow Volkswagen, there was no question. I saw him like an impressionist painting with blurred and undefined images, a forlorn, sodden figure waiting in the rain, and at that moment I knew it was the right thing to do.

He landed on the seat beside me and brushed the rain from his blonde hair. Then he grinned at me.

"Thanks."

I had offered him a lift, but with that smile and

those bright blue eyes, he could have anything he wanted.

"No problem," I lied

Of course I had a problem. Ninety-eight kilos of good-looking mystery and excitement sat beside me in a confined space. I was ready for it. He would be a welcome distraction from the purpose of my journey.

I checked the side mirror, making sure I didn't catch my eye – to have my organised, logical-self judge me back, would have undone everything - and I turned back onto the road.

"Where're you headed?" he asked.

"I'll take you to the bus terminal in Springfield."

"Terminal. Sounds final."

"Well, that's where your journey with me ends." I smiled a thin smile, just so he'd know I was friendly, usually.

He scanned the car. First over his shoulder to the back seat, then across the dashboard in front of him and over to me.

"Manual. You like to be in control."

I threw the stick back into top gear, acknowledging his observation.

Then he grabbed the disabled parking wallet from where it was attached to the front window.

"Andrew Ferguson." He raised a questioning eyebrow at me as he put it back.

"My brother."

"You are on your way to visit your disabled

brother."

"You're good." I smirked. "Anything else, Sherlock?"

"Your name's Carol."

"How –"

"Folder on the back seat."

I pushed my foot onto the accelerator. Bugger. Now he knows everything.

"You keep a tidy car, Carol. I can see nothing else about you. Even your clothes cover you entirely. Do you ever wear your hair down?"

What did he know? Denim jeans and a knitted jumper were about comfort and no, I always wore my hair up. Today the ribbon was for sentimental reasons.

"Could it be," he continued, "that your whole life is about disabled Andrew?"

I increased the pressure of my foot. The car responded with a satisfying roar. You haven't seen the crowbar under my seat.

"Have you ever helped someone?" I said aloud. "Or are you like a parasite, always hitching your next ride?"

"It's my mission to help people."

I scoffed and negotiated a bollard at the road works.

He had reached me. Ten minutes in and he had exposed the nerve and ripped away at my soul.

Didn't it always feel like it was me who did everything for Andrew? All the required paperwork that came with a minor in state care; all the visiting? Wasn't I the subject of those long, second glances when we were out in the community. They didn't think I heard their whispers of 'Maybe she's retarded too.' And wasn't it me who struggled with the determined ignorance of that same public when Andrew went into sensory overload?

But I was the one with the parking permit. They are transferrable, but that never occurred to Jake or Sally. And so for the second time this month, I was the one on the road to Sunnyside Villa.

Not me. Not today. I shuddered and put away my thoughts.

"You can find someone else. The bus stop will be crowded with the helpless."

He changed the subject.

"What is it you do, when you're not visiting?"

Well, in a small way had he changed the subject, but, Jeez, it was still about me. He'd already found my core, what else did he need to know? No way. I flipped it.

"You go first."

"Professional hitchhiker," he quipped.

Were we really the same? Not allowing anyone else in close? He was in my car. He was obliged.

"That's not fair."

"It's true."

"No one is a professional hitch hiker."

"I am."

I pushed down a gear to climb the hill. "Do you plan it?"

Did you stand on the kerb waiting for just the right victim?

He laughed then and I almost caught it and joined in. But laughter had been elusive for so long, it was like foreign territory and so I didn't venture there.

When I remained stoic, he calmed down and said, "No. I settle in for the ride and see where it takes me. You should try it some time."

"I don't do random."

The rain was loud now so we remained in silence but for the lashing at the windscreen. When the beat of the wipers had pounded my need to be known long enough, I said, "I'm a television director's assistant."

"Was that so hard?" He pulled out a packet of chewing gum, took a strip and held it toward me. I shook my head.

"Do you like it? The TV?"

I nodded. "Love it."

"I might know something about that. The show runs to a schedule, everything is timed to the second and the whole crew looks to you to keep it running smoothly."

"That's right. Not many people know how TV works, on the inside, in the studio, at least."

The clouds parted from above and watery sunshine lit the road ahead.

"We're nearly there and I don't even know your name."

"I'm Mark."

"I'm glad I gave you a lift, Mark. The company has been …illuminating. But this is it."

I breathed a sigh of relief as I pulled into the terminal car park. I left the engine running; this wouldn't take long.

"Come with me." He undid his seatbelt.

Oh yes, please. I can't take one more interminable visit. And you are quite dishy.

"What?!" I choked. "I can't do that. I have commitments, responsibilities."

He leant toward me. "Let's get on the next bus and see where it goes."

I giggled. The idea was absurd and oh, so captivating. Had I really rescued my own saviour from the rain this day?

He continued to make his case. "I'll even buy your ticket."

"No. Please get out."

"Not without you."

He reached across me and turned off the engine. Then he undid my seat belt. He could have been opening my blouse and I was letting him. He grinned and his blue eyes flashed as he released my hair and arranged it around my shoulders. He dropped the ribbon into my lap.

"You need to come with me." When he took my hand it was like he was caressing my neck.

"Yes. Yes, I do. But I can't." I shook my head and the feeling of my free hair surprised me.

He settled back into his seat. He didn't say anything and he didn't leave.

I fiddled with the ribbon in my hand, casually at first, but then I wound it around my palm, tighter and tighter until my fingers throbbed and discoloured.

It was me who got out. I bent to collect the crowbar and arrived at Mark's side of the car with it high on my shoulder.

"Go." I opened the door with my free hand.

"Nope."

I smacked the side of the car. Metal on metal. "Get out."

He was resolute, unflinching. I brought the crowbar down on the panel again and again. The car crumpled under my truncheon.

And then I saw it, there on the dashboard, the one thing that prevented me from catching a bus to wherever with Mark, the hitchhiker who wouldn't get out.

I smashed the window and dropped the crowbar. It clanged to the ground as I reached in through the broken glass to grab the plastic sleeve. With one tug, the permit inside was released. I tore it in half and then in half again and I continued ripping and tearing, scrunching and destroying until it lay in a wet, soggy mess in the puddle at my feet.

Then Mark emerged from my damaged car and we entered the bus terminal.

The sun was warm through the window when I stirred from sleep later in the afternoon. I stretched out my neck and rubbed my face.

"You look like you needed that." An elderly lady with a crinkled smile reached from her seat across the aisle and patted my hand.

Above the driver, a television monitor flickered to life. "Turn it up. Turn it up." Grasping the tops of seats, I pulled my way down the bus to get a closer view of the news report.

"Police are concerned for the safety of Carol Ferguson, whose vandalised car was found abandoned in this car park."

There, flickering before me at twenty-four frames a second, stood the bashed in testament to my apparent mental state.

And there was my sister, Sally. No doubt relishing her fifteen minutes of fame, she patted her hair and sobbed. "It's not like her. She never misses her visits with our brother."

She held a tissue to her eye then buried her head in Jake's shoulder. He put his arm around her and looked into the camera. "Please come home, Carol. We need you. Andrew needs you."

Not like me? Never miss a visit? Watch this.

I returned to my seat, scanning the passengers with a frown. Where was he? "Lose something, dear?" The old lady asked as I sat.

My mind apparently.

"I got on with someone. He seems to have disappeared."

"No. You were alone and you've been asleep since Springfield. Perhaps you were dreaming."

"No stops since then?"

She shook her purple, granny-dyed head. And then she said something that made me laugh out loud.

And I laughed until there was joy again. I laughed until I felt relief. And I laughed until I knew that Mark had known me because he was me and I had always known what I needed and would claim from this day on.

"Why don't you settle in for the ride and see where it takes you?"

CONTINUUM FOR URANIA

Helen Low

The bellbirds' song floats through the hills, an almost luminous sound, a silvery thread through the rich greens of the rain forest... a threaded memory. Frogs croak lugubriously in the creek below. A feral cat prowls, a dart of black through pale, hooded green orchids nodding above violets.

Today I met Jude, a potter. He gave me a lift to school when the car wouldn't start. He said, "I suppose you do have a life apart from walking in the rainforest, listening to bellbirds and teaching kids to make a noise?"

I told him of my dream, to write my concerto.

One of his pots is in the library—a mysterious piece, like a giant agate or opal, or a ball of molten glass.

He found me at school. "You forgot to leave me the car keys. It made no difference, I'm the resourceful type. I don't know why she wouldn't go for you. She started straight up for me."

"I wonder why?"

"You've got a lot to learn. Miss Forest." He drummed in time to Vivaldi. "What's the music?"

"Someone else's *Concerto for Flute*."

"I like it."

"Miss Forest has taken time from her concerto to find a poor potter."

"I've brought you some cassettes."

"I suppose I should offer you a drink? Come this way, Miss Celia Forest. Follow me."

A little room overlooking the gorge I mistook for his bathroom was a child's room with a gorgeous quilt on a hand-carved bed and a simple chair beside an armoire. I wondered why his wife could leave such precious possessions. Irena was foreign: Polish, or perhaps Czech, who spoke English beautifully. I heard her father was a university lecturer. She packed their bags and left.

Jude called to school and asked how my concerto

was progressing. How is it that I blurted out such a private dream to a stranger? I found myself playing for him, then we had tea.

He knows how much I love my days away from the city. He draws out my private thoughts in a way no one else has ever been able. He said he'd missed me; that he'd hoped to find someone who could fit into his way of life. He finds his cat insufficient company. He's picked me. How arrogant!

"You like it out here, don't you, Celia?"

"It's wonderful. These pots are fabulous."

"You might consider staying. Why don't you write your concerto here? If you can keep out of my way when I'm working."

"A time and place for everything? And everyone?"

"I don't like my woman underfoot."

"I have no intention of being your woman. Or your doormat."

"You must have thought of it or you wouldn't be here."

Jude phoned today. What was preventing my acceptance of his offer of a bed and board among the bellbirds?

"Common sense. I hardly know you."

He laughed. After a holiday spent in a grey

concrete box, I would see the error of my ways.

He called with a beautiful antique music stand. "All yours. I'll take it home. It will be waiting for you."

I can see it as I write, carved walnut stretchers in a lyre-shaped frame, mounted on an ebonised pedestal.

What had he used to persuade Irena?

I am happy here with Jude but always aware of her. Except in this little room where I practice and do my scribbling, there is little evidence she was ever here. This room was Helena's and overlooks the gulley. It appears to be as she left it, an oasis of feminine calm, her mother's Slavic origins all-pervasive.

The sparseness of the furnishings draws attention to their quality. The beautiful hand-hewn bed, the rich traditional stitchery of its quilt and the covers on the chair and dressing table, the painted nativity scene on the old wardrobe, shabby made beautiful by stencil, paint and wax.

Jude has kept this room in expectation of her return. He never speaks of Helena: a fleeting reference to Irena when it is unavoidable; hastily passed over, too painful to discuss.

I asked at the garage, also the agency for the post office and the bank. Dave said his wife knew Irena. She showed me a photo. "Here we are, Dave's birthday. That's Helena . That's Irena. They look like you, dark hair, pale skin. She was musical, too. She played the violin."

Tonight I made coffee and brought back some cake with the cups and saucers on the tray. "Did you like the cake?"

"Yes. It was good."

"It's sacher torte. A traditional recipe."

"I know. Don't make it again."

"It reminds you of her, doesn't it?"

"You knew it would."

Always Irena is here, just under the surface. Tonight I picked up my flute after dinner. I played a few notes, mimicking the bellbirds. Then, on a sudden impulse, perhaps simply to provoke, I blew a piercing crescendo, which drove Jude's cat out of the room. Jude turned in anger. "Put that thing away. It sounds like a banshee wail."

I have found a book of cuttings Jude has put aside; photos from his time at sea and press reports of sailors lost in an engine-room explosion. Irena had seen them, too: a sheet of manuscript paper in the book had her meticulous notation for a piece for violin.

Out of curiosity, I transposed it for flute. The thread of notes recalled the bellbirds and the mystery of the rainforest. The notes had a life of their own; seemingly without my conscious effort, the lines flowed from my pen.

I was compelled to complete the movement as a tribute to Irena. Never had I scripted with such ease. In just one afternoon the counterpoint developed, to flower and rise, to soar above her melodic phrases, the rich, rounded movement surprised me when I reproduced the inked notation.

Since I found her manuscript and played her music, Irena's presence is overwhelming. Would she approve of my arrangements of her air, which some strange force drove me to complete?

Yesterday I found letters from Poland, all unopened in a drawer in Jude's room.

Today I found her diary.

'Never have I experienced such heat! Jude took me with him up the hill to see the view to the furthest mountains. How strange this country is: the far hills wreathed mauve with smoke. Jude strode back down the hill, leaving me far behind. I found him at his wheel, still so full of energy. He worked through the night. Such pots! Pots as I have never seen before.

'Helena has been given a little kitten. Jude brought over a bowl he filled with milk - much too much for such a little one. Helena called him Nicholai. Jude finds time to talk to Nicholai but has no time for us. Each new pot is so wonderful! Some are great urns a small child could hide in. I read Helena the story of Ali Baba, and I said that perhaps the cave of Ali Baba looked like Jude's studio - enough pots for all the 40 thieves. Helena said it was a foolish story and no one would dare to hide in one of Jude's pots. Even Nicholai knows well enough to stay away.

'Yesterday Helena helped me paint our eggs. How beautiful she made them; marbled pink and orange, and violet and green. Nicholai has disappeared. We called 'Nicholai! Nicholai! late into the night, but still he didn't come. Helena breaks her heart for a lost black kitten.

'I make a new dress for Maritsa, her doll. I will embroider all the old designs, a sampler of many stitches. Today I wrote to my mother. She will be surprised that I sew. I preferred to read my books and play with my dolls. I asked mother if my Maritsa was still in my room.

'I told her Jude is always in his studio. So much of Jude is still a mystery. He appears casual but always he watches and knows where I have been and what I am thinking. He knows Helena thinks of her little Nicholai. He says he will get her another kitten, that a cat is a necessary member of a household. 'Even if there are no mice?' Helena asked.

'Jude has fired a kiln of rich, red glazed urns, a fine kiln of lustred pottery. We have our new Pushkin. A fine, furry fellow. Helena took Pushkin for a walk around the hill to see the view from her special place. Between the branches of the tree, one sees the thinning of the trees where the path dips down to the valley.

'Jude tells me he needs me here, but always he is too busy to talk to me and mother doesn't answer my letters. Helena senses this strangeness also but Nicholai felt it first of us all. Poor Nicholai.

How is it that I was not so wise? Nicholai would not choose a place by his side. Helena is always with her books, wishing to avoid his anger which comes so often now.

'I walked this morning while Jude fired the kiln. Helena came running so we went together. Jude works so hard, driven by his own creative force which has never been stronger but tomorrow he will take us for a picnic.

'The little church was ablaze when I woke this morning. Jude was already at the fire. He carries loads that other men can scarcely lift.'

I read Irena's thoughts and took my flute and lost myself in the sound. I wanted to find Irena, to reassure her, to tell her Jude missed her, that she was always on his mind, to beg her to return. I look at the music stand and see Irena. It was her music stand. And still is.

"Jude! I want to find Irena. I found her diary. It was in a drawer in Helena's wardrobe."

"She was just like you! Sitting, writing. Always

writing."

"When did she leave?"

"Who remembers? Some things I try to forget. You found a sheet of her music and brought her to life."

She is here! Across the valley, wisps of smoke from dying fires. I take a path through the bracken and the bellbirds' chimes are louder. I follow the track to where the old mineshafts are. A movement in the undergrowth: a black cat? I can't be sure. I see something that had been hidden in the bracken. Helena's doll.

Decomposed and the clothing all but disintegrated, I recognise Irena's stitching from the sampler in Helena's room; my study. She wouldn't have left without her doll…

I enquired at the bus station. The driver is certain he never picked up a beautiful dark haired woman with a rather quiet ten-year-old girl. I went to Jude, he refuses to talk. He is consumed by his pots.

I play my flute and clarinet. He tolerates my practising outside his studio; he says it even inspires him. I have completed my concerto, variations on Irena's melody, dedicated to Jude.

Irena has become an obsession.

Jude was firing pots large as amphorae when I went to find the answer. "I thought she and Helena went on the bus. The only thing I'm sure of was that when I got back from the fire, they had gone."

"The fire?"

"The church. It burned down. She'd gone too. She made her choice."

I love Jude, but tomorrow I must go. I will find another flat, but not in the city. What did Jude say? Grey people. Grey boxes. I must find Irena and her daughter if I can. I will never forget Jude. You can never be sure what's in people's minds but Jude always knows what I'm thinking.

"There you are, Celia. Hiding yourself away again. You need fresh air and exercise. Come with me to the top of the hill."

Jude fires his kiln again tonight.

He fires his kiln of golden pots and, in the centre, reaching to the arch his perfect creation; worthy of a Fire Princess or of Celia, his captive muse.

The brilliance and luminosity of its glaze is quite remarkable: when tapped, it rings, resounding with such a fluted, crystalline tone, one would swear a choir of angels and our bellbirds are singing together, accompanied by Celia, with wistful thread of sound from clarinet.

HIT POINTS
Duncan Richardson

The warriors stormed up the beach in a haze of swirling black and grey cloaks. Helmets gleamed in the sunlight. Swords and axes waved. Leather-clad feet dug into the wet sand, flinging it behind. Men beat their shields with their swords and called down curses on all who opposed them. Their screams froze my blood. Vikings!

Those around me slunk back, murmuring as the war band drew near. I looked at the empty ground around me, aching to run for the shelter of the crowd. The hairs on my neck prickled. The leader of the charging mob glared at me as I stood, alone and exposed. He pointed his sword at me and bellowed.

"Oh!" a woman behind me gasped.

I stared back at the warrior, trying to look calm. Maybe he was just trying to scare all of us.

"Aaiiiiiiii!" Another war band stormed into view up the beach. There was something almost friendly about their brown leather armour. A red and yellow banner carried by a tall man with a long beard streamed over their heads. Saxons. I breathed deeply. At last!

The Viking leader snorted and switched his attention to the Saxons who were now forming a shield wall. He pointed his sword at them and shouted something I couldn't understand. The Vikings charged past me in a clanking, yelling mass. My companions surged up behind me again, muttering. The warriors clashed, howling with rage.

A voice boomed from a speaker near the steps to the esplanade. "Parents, please keep children behind the safety tape while the battle is in progress."

I stepped back from the tape and pushed my hands into the warmth of my jacket pockets. The spectators moved towards the battle. I followed. The warriors had merged into a tangle of bodies. Swords flashed and clattered. Men tumbled, groaning. Others took their place but the Saxons shield wall was breaking. The Vikings crashed through.

The crowd pushed forward to get a better view but I hung back and looked at my watch. Nearly two o'clock. The café should be open. I could get a drink and try to work out why Roger, the Viking Leader, had glared at me. Perhaps he had heard what Jean said this morning, about me looking like a real Viking. Maybe he didn't like the way I laughed. I recalled his eyes, sharper than any of the fake weapons.

I ordered a coffee and a sandwich and sat by the café window overlooking the beach. A cappuccino machine whirred. I wondered how my attempt to make some kind of social life in the anonymity of London had led me into this position. I'd been expecting to meet fellow history buffs. Calm folk who liked a good argument and would never take it personally. How did I get it so wrong?

Below the edge of the footpath outside I could hear whoops of victory as the Vikings mopped up. The Saxons would get their act together later and beat the Vikings back, according to the program. I wasn't going to let Roger's pique stop me from seeing that.

Three months before, I'd seen an ad on a library noticeboard in west London, Historical Re-enactment and Wargames Club. I'd already tried the local amateur theatre but they were "So professional, darling" that I left after two meetings. And the hiking club members were heading up Mt

Everest and back on a long weekend. This could be my last attempt with groups.

On a cold, damp evening two nights later in the village hall, I met a tall, thin man wearing a blue jumper with Space Invaders characters on it. He was waving a sheet of paper and arguing with a round man in a faded leather jacket and pale, stained jeans.

"Hi," I said. "I'm Mark."

The thin man turned, his cheek twitching. "You must be the new recruit Simon mentioned. I'm Roger. This is Bruce. Our Hell's Angel."

Bruce raised his eyebrows and sighed. "Pleased to meet you." He held out his tattooed hand. I was expecting a bone-crusher. Instead, his handshake was firm.

I held out my hand to Roger.

"Ah, I just salute." He swung his arm across his chest.

I blinked at Bruce.

He shrugged. "Don't worry," he said. "Roger thinks he's a Viking. But really he's an accountant."

"I don't," snapped Roger, flourishing the rule sheet. "You're always exaggerating. Just like you do with hit points. Anyway, what's wrong with accountants?"

"Where shall I begin?" said Bruce and grinned. "Some people get carried away. Occasionally."

I slid away and wandered on, into the fug of an overheated room, full of damp anoraks and tweed jackets.

A man with a mass of curly brown hair and gold-rimmed glasses approached me, holding a cup of tea. "You must be our new Aussie," he said. "I'm Simon. Club President. Welcome."

I shook his hand. It was warm from the cup.

"I'm into the Ancients. What's your thing?"

"A bit of everything," I replied.

He frowned. "That must be expensive."

I nodded. "I like variety."

He turned his head slightly, like a startled squirrel. "Have you done any re-enacting?" he said.

"Nope." I'd seen some. Overweight men marching in a field, pretending to be Romans.

"You've got a treat in store then," said Simon.

When the formal meeting started, Simon welcomed me officially in a separate agenda item, despite Roger's quibble about a point of order. Simon beamed at me as if I were his own creation.

Over the next few weeks, I played a few table-top games and slowly learned the rules the club used. As we packed up one evening, Simon asked if I wanted to join them at a weekend event in Margate. Table games would be played inside a large hall and historical re-enactments battled out on the beach. We'd share a minibus and a cheap B&B.

We met after work the following Friday. I was in the back of the minibus with Roger and his girlfriend Jean. She was sandwiched between us. I felt her warmth, trying not to be so aware of it. Simon drove, his wife Helen beside him.

"Now please, Simon," Helen said as we hit the motorway, "don't make your Helen of Troy joke just for Mark's benefit." She looked back at me and as we passed under a street light, I caught a glint in her eye.

Simon laughed. "I don't need to now."

Jean turned to me. "Simon reckons he could only have married a Helen." She sighed. "And Roger calls me Brunhilda sometimes. When he gets his blood up."

Silence. Then everyone laughed. Except for Roger who hissed in the darkness.

"What?" said Simon. "Not mumbling your Old Norse curses again are you?" He chuckled, half turning.

I tried not to look at Roger but then worried he might think I was shunning him. My skin chilled. What kind of weekend was this going to be?

Next morning, we gathered in a 1920s dance hall, converted into a conference centre next to the beach. Tables and stalls spread from wall to wall. I gazed at the ceiling, painted blue with clouds and brightly-coloured balloons and biplanes. A pang of nostalgia hit me. This place was built for dancing. Not men in stripy jumpers, playing with toy soldiers on table tops. I tried to imagine the romance that must've bloomed there decades ago, the lives changed by luck or perseverance. The painted sky was bluer than the real one, powdery, thick and soft.

"That's what I like to see," said Helen, appearing beside me. "A man enjoying the scenery."

I looked at her. Her mouth and eyebrows were turned up.

"Yeah," I said. "I like the art deco stuff." I pointed to the gold ornamentation around the stage.

"Yep." Helen swung her eyes over it as she edged closer to me. "I like these places too. But Mark, I'm a bit of a 'conference widow', if you get my meaning."

"Hmm," I said.

She smiled wryly and slid into the crowd. I wanted to follow her but held back. She's married, I thought. She's just playing games.

I wandered through the growing crowd, spotting Bruce, the "Hells Angel". He'd ridden his motorbike down, rumbling in late. He was wearing his dull leathers, his eyes intent on the game, looking more like a meditating Buddha than a menace to society.

I perched on a metal chair by a large table covered with a green cloth. Plastic buildings, trees and papier maché hills dotted the landscape. Miniature ancient armies clashed in silence except for the click of colliding dice, the clink of Bruce's chains and the odd grunt of despair. Simon's Greeks were attacking Trojans controlled by Roger. Bruce was an umpire. Roger was doing most of the grunting. Jean stood next to him, screwing up her face. It looked like amusement. She shrugged, glanced around and sidled over to Bruce. Roger didn't seem to notice.

I scanned the table, admiring the paintwork on the warriors.

"Where's Helen of Troy?" I said.

"Huh," mumbled Roger. "We don't need her."

Simon smiled. "A model in this scale could never do her justice. She was too beautiful." He sighed.

Bruce raised his eyebrows at me. The battle continued. I lost interest. I looked at Simon, his pointy nose and chin shining. He's all wrapped up in a fantasy, I thought. He doesn't appreciate his real Helen.

I pushed my chair back, the rusty legs scrawping on the timber floor.

"Don't worry," said Helen, pulling up a chair beside me. "You'll get the next game."

I shrugged. "Not worried. I'm not a fanatic."

"Hmmm. Really?"

I glanced at her. Across the table, Simon grinned and blew a kiss to Helen. She laughed.

Simon leant forward, measuring an advance of his troops with a ruler.

I stole a glance at Helen's ear, pale and perfect

like a sculpted shell.

"Here come the chariots," she said softly.

Her purr sent shivers down my neck. Maybe I'd got this all wrong, I thought. Was it one of those swingers' groups I'd read about, masquerading as a military history club? Did the dressing up and role play add spice to their orgies? My head buzzed.

"Is this a private chat or can anyone join in?" Jean pulled up a chair without waiting for an answer. She smiled at me. "Mark, I bet you're itching to get into it."

Helen chuckled, putting a hand over her mouth. "Aren't we all?"

"I'm not worried," I said. "I'm just as happy to chat."

"Oh, a ladies' man," said Jean, patting my arm.

"Really?" said Helen. She raised an eyebrow. Her mouth twitched.

My face felt hot.

Jean beamed at me. "I thought Aussie blokes liked their mates' company best."

Helen's face dissolved into quiet laughter.

It was hard to keep a straight face as I turned to Jean. "Well, I'm only half Australian."

"What's the other half?" Her eyes narrowed.

Helen said, "Do tell."

"You know," said Jean. "You'd make a good Viking. You've got the right hands. Why don't you try on some of the gear?"

"Yes," said Helen, rubbing her fingers together. "We'll help you."

"You can't do that!" It was Roger.

I glanced up, feeling cold suddenly. Roger was pointing at Simon. Just another game dispute.

I took a deep breath and stood. It would be all right, I thought. Jean would be a chaperone. "OK. Let's go."

They led me to a large marquee on the beach and after a long search for the right sized helmet, I was fully kitted out in leather breast plate, helmet, cloak and sword. We stepped outside.

"Now that's a real Viking," said Jean.

Helen giggled. My face burned and I looked around for a distraction. A loose crowd of Viking warriors was heading our way. Roger was at the front, his face a crude mask of loathing.

"Oh," said Helen.

Jean turned. "He'll be fine. He's got a battle soon."

I ducked into the tent, shed my gear and escaped under the back wall while Helen and Jean greeted the others. I heard Roger's raised voice but it was muffled by the banter of others.

A crowd was gathering half way down the beach and I joined them. It was a large crowd so I didn't see Roger lead his Vikings to the water's edge. I heard them start their war cries and despite some misgivings, I shuffled forward to get a better view. That was when Roger spotted me.

So I retreated to the café before the first battle was over. When I finished my coffee and returned for part two, the Saxons had their victory. Even Roger was 'killed' and I found myself hoping he would stay that way but he got to his feet and strode towards me. I spotted Jean and Simon in the crowd behind him.

"In the name of my father, Erik Bloodaxe," Roger roared, "and his father, Bjorn Quickblade, I challenge you, Mark of the South, to a duel. Do you accept? Or will you flee like a cur and be banished forever?"

An elderly man clapped. "Hey, I thought it was over? These chaps are good aren't they?" He pointed at me. "But why's he not in costume?"

Simon frowned and rubbed his chin.

"Hey," said Jean. "This is getting exciting."

"Well?" barked Roger. "What do you say?"

I took a deep breath. "Let's discuss this. There's nothing to fight about."

Roger sneered, his nostrils twitching. "The time for talk is over Mark Lily Liver. Get your weapons and meet me here..." He peered at the headland. "...when the sun is between yonder hills. We will settle this like men."

People cheered.

I pointed at Simon. "Why aren't you stopping him?"

He shrugged.

Roger's face crinkled as he shed his Viking

persona and became again a disgruntled accountant. He snarled, "Simon only wanted you in the club so we could get a council grant. He needed a third nationality and you were it."

I groaned. "I'm not after Jean," I said. "It's…" Helen's the one I want, I thought. But I couldn't say that. Not yet. Simon doesn't deserve her. I deserved her. I wouldn't make her spend weekends as a bored spectator to war games. I'd devote myself to her. I'd to kiss her alabaster neck and gaze into those eyes.

And I wanted to strike Simon down to prove it.

But what if she laughed?

My resolve faded. I headed for the esplanade without looking back.

As I walked, I tried to clear my head. I could catch the first train back to London and never see those crazy people again. Roger couldn't roam the streets looking for me, armed to the teeth…

He wouldn't need to. Simon, being a solid businessman, had the membership list up to date. With my address.

I could go back to the café.

I could walk out on the pier.

Or I could explore the streets of Margate. Roger would have to leave me alone. His inner accountant would never let him attack me in the street.

I spotted Helen ahead of me at the top of some steps to the beach about fifty metres away. She seemed to be gazing out to sea. The wind caught her hair and she folded her arms against the cold. I longed to hold her, to keep her warm forever.

All my resolve to escape evaporated. I strode towards her. What would make her leave Simon the smug pharmacist to be with me, an aimless Arts Graduate temporarily employed as a low-level clerk?

"Helen!" I called. But the wind took my words away.

She started walking down the steps, her arms out beside her for balance. I wanted to take her hand. I ran to the top of the steps. She walked over the sand towards the water. Some of the crowd were still there, mingling with the re-enactors, trying on helmets or waving swords. I scurried down, trying to keep her in view as she mingled with the crowd.

By the time we reached the wet, hard sand, she was only just ahead of me but my throat was so dry I couldn't call out. I didn't know what to say. Helen ducked sideways between some people and as I tried to follow, I found myself in a clear space.

"Arrrr!" bellowed Roger. "Vengeance at last!" Pale sunlight glinted on the axe he held by his side.

I held up my hands, not in surrender. Like two stop signs. "You're mad. I told you, I'm not trying to steal Jean."

"No." It came from my behind and it sounded like Jean. Roger lurched towards me.

"Where's your weapon?" he yelled.

"I don't have one. Come on. Let's go to the pub and forget about this. It's just a misunderstanding."

He swung his axe. "By Odin, I'll not listen to such talk! Will someone arm this weakling before I throw honour aside and wreak vengeance on his vile body?"

Something cold was being pressed into my hand. A sword. I glanced up. Simon. What the..? Did he know I wanted Helen after all? Was he setting up Roger to do his dirty work? That cool gleam in his eye…

Roger danced towards me, large and malevolent against the blurred background of spectators. A few paces away, he halted, digging his toes into the damp sand and swinging his axe down. It bit it deep into the beach.

"Hey, I thought that was fake," someone said.

So had I. I touched a finger to my sword, feeling the bite of a real blade. I searched the crowd for Simon but he had vanished. Did he want us both dead? Anger surged through my body. I'll show him. I'll show Helen too. I'll beat this maniac and take her away from all this.

Roger tugged his axe out of the sand and leapt at me. I brought my sword up to parry and felt the juddering blow.

The crowd cheered.

"Ladies and gentlemen," said the loudspeaker. "Here we see axe versus sword. A classic example of warriors meeting in single combat." It was Simon! What the hell?

Roger darted left, saliva dripping down his chin. I focussed on his hands. Mine gripped my sword handle, trying to adjust to its weight, holding it sideways at waist height.

"Slave!" roared Roger, foam flying from his lips. He sprang, axe raised. I watched, timing its fall, ready to parry. My right foot slid in the wet sand. I fell on my back. The axe was plummeting towards my throat.

I rolled sideways.

The axe cut the sand. I swung my blade and swiped Roger hard across his armoured belly. It felt good and my arms tingled, ready to strike again.

"Argh!" Roger staggered sideways, his axe tumbling away.

An engine roared and the crowd parted as a large black motorbike nosed its way through. Bruce glanced around, grinning. A smiling Jean was riding pillion, her arms wrapped around his waist.

"We're off now folks," Bruce said. "So no bloodshed needed."

He revved the motor, pulled down his visor and they rolled forward. "Now this is a real Viking," shouted Jean, pointing to Bruce. The crowd parted before them. Some people smiled, or laughed, others gaped and scratched their heads.

Roger rubbed his chin, loosening his fake

beard. I peered into the spectators. Where was Helen?

Simon leant over me, his face blank. "To quote the Iron Duke, 'That was a close run thing.'"

"You're all mad," I said.

He shook his head, lips pursed. "I'm not Menelaus, you know. And you're never going to be Paris."

I stood, leaving the sword on the ground, then shook the sand off my hands and strode away. That was it. Back to London and my lonely flat. I was finished with groups.

NAUGHTY ZOMBIES

Jodie Lane

It was a dark but not-quite-stormy night as the wind whipped through the trees and grey clouds scudded across the sky. The park gate creaked on its hinges. In the playground, swings swayed back and forth with a quiet screech over dry grass. A late night jogger paused at the gate and considered doing a quick lap of the park, but the dark shadows of the trees moving in the wind gave the impression the place was not *quite* deserted. The jogger pressed on, suddenly eager to be home and behind closed doors.

The wind dropped and a bone-chilling muttering could be heard.

"Brains... Brains..."

Several shadows emerged from the trees and

lurched towards the playground. The sound of shuffling feet and morbid groaning echoed through the night.

"Brains... *Brains!*"

Cough. A petulant voice interrupted. "Why does it always have to be brains?"

"*Brai*-- what?"

The petulance decreased as the speaker tried to take on a reasonable tone. "I said, why does it always have to be brains? I mean, there are plenty of other parts to a person. Legs and arms and other bits and pieces. Saying 'brains' is a bit boring after awhile."

The shuffling and groaning stopped and an embarrassed silence grew.

"I'm just saying." A defensive mutter.

An exasperated huff came in reply. "We're zombies. 'Brains' is what we say!"

Another voice interjected. "She's got a point, Greg. I know I get a bit tired of saying 'brains' all the time."

Greg spluttered with indignation. "What is this, a bloody committee? We've always said 'brains'-- that's how people know we're zombies. If we didn't say 'brains' they'd just think we were drunks and tell us to piss off!" Someone tried to respond but he rode over the top of them. "And how can you be tired? You're undead!"

Cough. "Figure of speech, Greg."

"Anyway, no one is going to mistake us for

drunks," the first protester added. "Not once we start ripping limbs off. It's not even like we eat *just* brains. We'll sink our teeth into anything."

"Yeah, Greg," another voice chimed in. "And if they do think we're drunks, it just lets us get closer to them. People watch a lot of zombie shows these days. They twig pretty early, then leg it."

A murmur of agreement went through the group. "It sure is hard to catch anyone when all you can do is shuffle."

"Mmm."

"Yeah."

Yet another voice chimed in. "Why can't we move a bit faster, anyway? Plenty of movies have zombies that run and even jump these days. And I'm not just talking about the classic 'jump-scare' that Doreen here has perfected."

Respectful nods ensued, albeit slightly carefully in the case of those whose heads were only attached with sinews of grey, rotting skin. Everyone knew zombies were famous for jump-scares, but it was a lot harder than it looked. Even lurching took a lot of practice, to get the forward-yet-sideways motion just so. Many zombies had put their hips out dragging legs at awkward angles.

"Yes, well, I'm sure Doreen is to be congratulated for practising so hard, but the point is, we shuffle, and we say 'brains!' because that's what zombies do! It's traditional!" Greg sounded a bit snarky. He had been known to run morning classes on the correct intonation of 'brains'.

"Don't get worked up, Greg," one voice said soothingly.

"I'm not getting worked up!" he snapped. "I just don't see why this has suddenly turned into a bloody Round-Table discussion of appropriate zombie behaviour!"

This time, the awkward silence was broken by Doreen's voice piping up; "We just want to try something different, Greg. That's all." She trailed off uncertainly.

"We? Who's we?" he demanded. "Come on, you lot have been talking about this behind my back, haven't you?"

Shuffle, shuffle.

"Fine. Just fine! Do what you like then! Forget tradition and correct zombie —"

"Greg, I really do think you are overreacting just a little," the soother's voice said. "We just want to have a little fun."

"Fun? What do you mean, fun? The hell with fun."

Several minutes later one of the others finally spoke. "Would have had a bit more impact if he'd stormed off. The shuffle just doesn't have the same effect when you're trying to make a dramatic exit."

Several heads shook sadly. "Poor old Greg, he really is committed to tradition."

"Bugger tradition," the voice that had

complained about the slowness of shuffling continued. "Haven't you seen World War Z? Those bastards can *move*. The old shuffling zombie that groans and mutters 'brains' is on its way out. We've got to get with the times."

Everyone murmured in agreement.

"Does that mean we can say what we like now?" Doreen wanted to know.

"Well, I am," the voice that had sparked the whole debate sounded defiant. "If I want to say 'legs' or 'ears' I will!"

"Arms..."

"Feet..."

"Elbows..."

They considered this. "Maybe not 'elbows'," someone said. "Sounds a bit odd."

"What about 'bum'?" someone else wanted to know. A nervous titter was heard.

"Heehee. Or 'boobs'?" chimed in another. Chuckles spread through the group. Others started coming up with suggestions of their own.

"Willy!"

"Tits!"

"Fanny!"

The cries got more raucous as the zombies poured out of the park, sprinting down the road and leaping onto cars. By morning the infestation had spread through the city, and zombies would never be the same again.

THE GREAT HOU-DIMWIT

Alicia Bruzzone

"I'm going to make the lighthouse disappear."

My brother's face is overjoyed and I'm sure most older sisters would find it infectious. I don't anymore. Sure, at age ten it was cute when he wore a checked tea towel as a cape. Not so much now he's sixteen.

I turn my attention back to the dishes I'm washing and he's meant to be drying. "You can't make an ace disappear from a deck of cards, how are you going to get rid of an entire lighthouse, Caleb?"

My brother, while enthusiastic, lacks any actual magical talent. Most people would see their excessive list of continual failures and think perhaps they should consider an alternate profession. Not Caleb.

"I'm getting in character. You have to use my stage name. I'll be performing for you tonight."

"What sort of a stage name is Lester?" I exclaim while throwing my hands in the air. Suds fly off my soapy fingers and stick to the laminate kitchen cabinets. It doesn't matter how many times we have this conversation; Caleb's choice of stage name makes no sense.

"The greatest magician ever went by Harry," he replies sternly. "And his real name was Erik."

I tap my fingers in annoyance on the counter before grabbing more dirty plates. He's telling the truth; Caleb has supplied me with more Harry Houdini trivia than any self-respecting teenage girl would ever admit to knowing. Not if she wanted friends, anyway. What he's deliberately omitting is the fact Harry was a mishearing of 'Ehrie,' a pet name for Erik, that earned him the misnomer. "Fine, Lester. But you still can't make the lighthouse disappear." And not only because it was heritage listed.

"I figured it out!" he protests as he blocks my path to the sink. Caleb's arched eyebrows and wide pupils make him look ten years old again. That was when his obsession started and everyone said it was just a phase. "Come on, Cassie," he pleads.

I give in, because if he finally has got something to work, I want to be the one to see it. I stopped letting him cut me in half years back but I can spectate without requiring stitches. Hopefully. Besides, he'll finish the dinner dishes faster if he wants to be somewhere.

Shoving him to the side, I plonk the next load of dishes into the warm water fingers wrinkling as I scrub off mashed potato remnants. "I'll drive us out there once we're done," I concede.

As predicted, Caleb starts swiping with vigour, his tea towelled hand outstretched as he impatiently waits for me to catch up. "We've gotta take Birdie," he reminds me. My shoulders sag as I pull the plug.

I know. Believe me, I know.

Birdie used to be a classic white vehicle with red striping. Birdie is now a rust bucket on wheels that somehow turned cream over the years… with no air conditioning. In spring this didn't bother me so much but it's now summer. Seven o'clock and the sun beats ferociously. Until we get to the coast there's barely a hint of breeze; which means windows down, mosquitos in.

Caleb, I mean Lester, bought Birdie to complete his magic act. He found a secret compartment under the boot carpet that to him signalled destiny, and spent every cent of birthday money, pocket money and fast food earnings when he turned sixteen. The dimwit can't drive it yet but he lets me borrow it from time to time. It's handy if I want to find myself ostracised from every social gathering ever.

Birdie's backseat is currently dominated by dark bed sheets, metal rods and a plethora of other items I think I'm not meant to see. Any bet Lester has me close my eyes and tries to lasso the black sheets over the top.

My thoughts are interrupted as I struggle to pull Birdie into second, her engine spluttering as the automatic choke threatens to drop out the bottom of the car. You know she's nearing her deathbed when the noise of the engine idling manages to drown out the roar of the cicadas. With luck, Birdie will take a handful of mozzies down with her when the engine inevitably gives in. I slap another annoying insect off my arm.

It takes manoeuvring but I eventually roll Birdie into the lighthouse car park overlooking the inlet.

"You can't park here," Caleb tells me, a little of his sparkle gone as his head darts around, looking out the windows. "You need to park on the street." He checks his watch as I plug in my seatbelt.

Complaining as I get Birdie to turn over, I execute a seven point turn due to the lack of power steering before resting her heavy wheels in the gutter on the other side of the road. "Better, oh great and powerful Lester?"

Caleb glances at the time on his wrist again. "You need to stay here for seven to eight minutes.

Then I shall make the lighthouse disappear!" He waves his hands theatrically but it's his mouth I'm watching. His grin stretches long enough to go through three postcodes.

He exits with an armload of junk from the backseat, leaving me to watch the fading sun paint the sky a brilliant mash of colours that fade with every passing minute. The cicadas seize the moment the sun drops from the sky to form their constant thrum into a crescendo, the buzz worse than the static feedback when attempting to use Birdie's radio. The lighthouse is still standing, so whatever Caleb is planning he either hasn't done it yet or it didn't work. I'm going with option number two.

Caleb's head pops down to my window. "See the lighthouse?" he asks, his hands swept to the side as he presents it to me out the window.

"Nope," I reply sarcastically.

He doesn't give in. "When the timer goes off on this phone in twenty minutes," Caleb leans in and drops his mobile on the console next to me, "I shall make it disappear. Boom, swish, vanished!" He puts on the expression I long ago dubbed his 'magician face'. Not because it resembles a magician, but because he uses it when he's pretending. I think he looks like a slightly squished cane toad but Lester isn't a good name for an amphibian. Or anything else for that matter.

"I am prepared to be dazzled," I say, looking

back out the window to the lighthouse. Twenty minutes; at least he isn't planning to remove it brick by brick.

Caleb taps me on the shoulder. He has a sheepish look on his face as he rubs the back of his neck. "You can't look. Not until the timer goes off."

My mouth twitches at the sides, threatening to laugh. I can't do that, not yet anyway. Once the actual failure has been accomplished, then maybe I'll indulge. Until that point, I need to remain semi-supportive. Nodding in acknowledgement, I fish around my bag for my phone; the perfect time wasting device.

Eighteen minutes later and Caleb is lunging in my window, his body licked with sweat as he scrambles for his phone. He taps in a rush, fingers flying over the screen as his breath comes out in heavy pants. Dashing off without a word, curiosity piques at me more than the desire to play another level of Candy Crush. The timer on his phone now says twelve minutes. Caleb always was optimistic.

With the setting sun, the heat isn't as stifling, though my legs still stick with sweat to Birdie's upholstery. Despite the tedious boredom, I don't peek towards the lighthouse. Part of me desperately wants to be surprised when this trick is over. It'd be nice if my brother pulled something off, though I still think he should have done some small scale testing before moving onto making an entire lighthouse disappear. Lighthouses tended to stick out. It was kind of the point.

My heart races when his face pops in the window next to me, startled by the sudden appearance. The timer hasn't gone off yet.

"Prepare to be astounded!" Caleb announces, now completely in character. He reaches across me to retrieve his phone. Something clunks as he gropes around uselessly, and I hold back from telling him to use the stupid passenger door. You can't argue with 'Lester' or he tries to pull coins out of your ears and pour disappearing milk into your lap. Last time I had to get five cents removed from my nostril by a doctor while wearing milk-sodden pants.

Caleb opens the door for me and I realise how dark it has become. After waiting for my eyes to adjust I check to see if he has indeed made a lighthouse disappear. There is nothing that could hold back my peal of laughter. "It took you half an hour for that?"

Caleb folds his arms as I cross the road to the lighthouse lot. "It would have been faster if I had an assistant to help."

"Help do what? You strung up two black bed sheets as a curtain."

Caleb examined his handiwork. It looked worse than the time he'd strung the Christmas lights. He must have attached wires somewhere and heaved the flimsy fabric to the same height as the lighthouse. It might be more believable if it weren't billowing and at an odd angle. Also, if the lighthouse wasn't operational. Edges of white poked through the weave of the fabric.

"I can still see the lighthouse."

I think Caleb might have protested if not for the strong gust of wind that blew the sheet back onto itself in a folded mess on the wire.

"Hey, you invented a pretty good camping clothesline," I offer by way of commiseration when I see the disappointment on his face and the way his shoulders stoop.

Caleb kicks at a nearby stone and tells me to head back to the car.

Turning, I peer at the other side of the road where I left Birdie. She isn't there. Birdie isn't the sort of car to go unnoticed and everyone within a kilometre would have heard her engine being switched on if she were stolen. It takes me a moment to figure it out as I stand frozen and mute staring at the spot.

This was Caleb's trick. He made the car disappear.

Emotions flood me as I screech a whoop of glee and rush Caleb into a hug. "You finally did it! You did it! I didn't notice a thing and I was in there the whole time! That was amazing!" I'm jumping and squealing like an idiot but I don't care. Caleb is finally capable of performing a magic trick. And it was awesome!

When I let him go and take a step back, Caleb's

face is red. He scrubs the back of his neck and takes a small bow.

He isn't smiling.

I don't understand.

"For my final trick, you need to look over there," Caleb cries, pointing to the ocean as he takes off running in the opposite direction. I watch him instead.

A gleam of white roof creeps under a streetlight, slowly rolling down the incline. Birdie has gone free range.

Recalling Caleb's earlier fumbling to retrieve his phone, I take in a huge gulp of air so I can yell. "You bumped the handbrake, didn't you?" This isn't part of the show.

Welcome to life with the Great Hou-dimwit.

SQUIRE'S CHAMPIONSHIP

Kasper Beaumont

The sword flew time and time again, cutting the torso to ribbons.

"My Lord Varnon, are you prepared for the tournament?"

"Indeed, friend Marlan. It has occupied my every thought this past month."

Varnon wiped a gloved hand across his sweaty brow and gritted his teeth as he attacked the training dummy again.

"The young lady yonder is observing you, my Lord."

"I am well aware of Miss Elsabet's presence, Marlon. Frustration at her watching me only spurs me on. I have no time for a dalliance with a pretty lady when I must win this tournament and prove my worth to the realm. Becoming a knight is my only goal." His lips were tight as he concentrated on his sword, although his eyes did dart across to where she watched him with a love-struck smile upon her face. She waved a white handkerchief and he groaned and turned away.

Marlan gave a cough which may have been hiding a smile. "Would you mind if I were to seek her affections then?"

The head of the dummy flew across the field and Varnon looked at his sword with wide eyes. "How unexpected!" He scratched his blond hair and tied it at the back with a band. "Come Marlan, we must be getting to our armour. What is your first challenge?"

Marlan grinned in Elsabet's direction. "Pike skills."

"Mine is the sword. There are likely to be over one hundred squires competing today, so if I do not see you, best of luck."

"You too, my Lord." The two young men clasped wrists in the Diagro fashion and headed to the preparation marquees. Varnon was in the royal marquee with servants to dress him and Marlan was in his family's tent. There was also a large commoners' marquee for those without provisions. The ways of the Diagro peoples were such that every man was encouraged to become a knight when they turned eighteen. Some had to endure the trials more than once to pass, and to be the champion of the tourney was a guarantee to become one of the king's elite guards. For Varnon, the ambitious prince of the Diagro Plains, anything less than first would be a failure.

Varnon's strength was his swordsmanship and the first trial was over for him in a blink. He disarmed all three of his opponents in rapid succession and they lay gasping on the ground as he bowed to the royal box. He was pleased to receive a wave from his father, but as his gaze travelled along the stands, he was a little disappointed not to see Elsabet watching him. He sighed.

However, the maiden was soon forgotten in the pike agility skills challenge.

This was a learned routine wearing jerkins and hose. Varnon always found it a struggle when the squires dug the pike into the ground and spun around, kicking at the practice dummies while rotating through the air. Varnon's broad shoulders and heavy muscles seemed to work against him in this challenge and he stumbled as his pike moved in the ground. He only hit two of the three targets.

The pike skills were won by a slender boy Varnon had never met with a dirty face, ragged clothes and a knitted cap which Varnon thought looked ridiculous. Despite his looks, he was quick and agile on his feet and finished the challenge first with the highest score from the three judging knights. *I cannot believe this pauper beat me.* Varnon's face reddened at being beaten. He pushed up his sleeves and resolved to work even harder in the remaining two challenges.

Archery was next and this was a hotly contested event. Of the thirty squires in Varnon's group, five won their way into the shortlist to compete for the winning title. Four were local high-born lads with whom Varnon was acquainted, but he screwed up his nose to see that the last was the dirty lad named Warrel, who had won the pike challenge. *Him again.*

Varnon knuckled down and fired the best shots he had ever made in his life, but Warrel matched him arrow for arrow. The other three competitors were eliminated and it was down to two. The other groups had finished their rounds and watched the contest while awaiting their last rotation. Warrel concentrated hard and seldom met Varnon's eye, while the prince became flush with embarrassment at being unable to defeat him. The targets were moved back another twenty paces and both squires fired their arrows. Again their arrows both hit the red inner circles. Varnon clenched his fists around the bow and arrows and scowled at the stranger's prowess.

"Hear ye, hear ye, this archery round has been named a draw between Prince Varnon of Varx Castle and Warrel of Noble River Town." The herald's call was met with murmurs of disappointment, but the crowds split up again and proceeded to the final round. Varnon's group had the highest scores thus far and most of the crowd followed them. According to the tally board, Varnon was in the lead, but there were still three squires who could beat him if they landed a clean lance on his breastplate, and unhorsed him in the joust. One of those was Warrel, who had won the pike and tied for the archery.

Varnon's eyes burrowed into the back of Warrel's dented armour which had been scrounged from the commoners' tent. *No commoner is going to be the winner of this tourney.*

The squires were assigned jousting partners for two passes apiece. The jousting pikes were blunt wood and won a score apiece for either hitting the breastplate or unhorsing the opponent.

Jousting was the least practised skill for most squires, due to the high risk of injury.

Varnon gave a smile of satisfaction to see that some squires had poor riding skills and one was even thrown from a wide-eyed horse before the challenge commenced. He frowned to see that the annoying Warrel seemed a competent rider, even when given a horse which reared up, the lithe boy held on tight and kept his seat. Varnon sniffed but did feel a certain admiration for the nerve of this chap who had probably had little access to the professional joust trainers that he himself had at the castle.

Even so, Varnon would not show mercy to this

competitor who threatened his chances of winning. He watched as Warrel made both his passes. The first pass, neither competitor scored, then on the second pass, Warrel's lance touched the breastplate for a moment before the lance of the other squire pushed Warrel to the ground. The knight lay there panting and two servants helped the lad to his feet in the heavy armour.

Varnon nodded and mounted his horse. To his advantage, he was familiar with this horse, a black destrier which belonged to his knight, Sir Rawlan. The horse nickered in greeting before its eyes hardened and he pulled at the bit. Both horse and squire were breathing heavily. Varnon gathered the reins tight in his shield hand and dug in his spurs. On the first pass, he hit his opponent's shield hard and the squire was thrown from his horse. He landed hard and was carried moaning from the field. Varnon clenched his fist but turned away so as not to show the uncertainty that flashed across his eyes.

On the second pass, both Varnon and his opponent scored a point when both lances touched breastplates a split second before the poles crossed and contact was broken. Neither was unhorsed and both lads lifted their visors and smiled to offer encouragement. The crowd cheered.

A trumpet blew. "Hear ye, hear ye. The concluding round of the day will be between the two highest scorers to determine the overall Squire

Champion. Our two finalists are Prince Varnon of Varx Castle …" He raised a shiny gauntlet in the air and the crowd cheered. "… And Warrel of Noble River." A pin could have been heard dropping in the arena as the squire with the dented armour shuffled his feet and looked at the dirt.

"Come on Warrel, show your courage, man." Varnon clanked his shoulder into the squire's and the boy flinched. He could see the whites of Warrel's eyes behind his visor and thought he also detected a tremble. The horses were brought to them and they mounted to rousing cheers. Varnon's name was chanted around the lists and the king could be seen smiling broadly.

The squires raised their lances in salute and galloped to either end of the barrier. They stared each other down while waiting for the flag. Varnon launched a second before Warrel, then both approached at full gallop toward the impact. There was a crash of splintered wood as Varnon's lance shattered on Warrel's breastplate, denting the armour further into the lad's chest and sending him flying through the air before a sickening crash onto the compacted dirt below.

The crowd fell silent and the stretcher bearers rushed forward. Varnon leapt off his horse and rather than celebrate his victory, his eyes widened with concern. He tore off his visor and raced to Warrel's side. "How fares he?"

His friend Marlan appeared at his side and they

ran the last few steps together. "My Lord, there is something you must know. Warrel is …" The words caught in Marlan's throat as Warrels' visor was removed and long blonde hair fell in waves around Elsabet's pretty face that was smeared with dirt.

Varnon's mouth dropped open with shock. "No … it cannot be. A lady could never have competed so well in the trials. What sorcery is this?"

Elsabet's big eyes opened and she blinked back tears of pain. "It was the only way for you to notice me, my Lord." Her breath came in ragged gasps and her teeth clenched as pain racked through her.

"Oh, my brave Lady. You have proved such a commendable opponent. I wish with all my heart for you to be well so that I might prove worthy of you."

Cheers of surprise and delight echoed around the stands as he placed a gentle hand on her cheek and kissed her.

TWO CAN PLAY GAMES
David Tofts

I was staring at the pages of my woman's magazine, but my eyes had stopped scanning the words. As the Sydney Express cut its way through the rain, I thought about the impending interview and what kind of jumped-up little shit I'd have to smile at and be pleasant to. I wondered if I could do 'pleasant'. I had a seat by the window, watching the places I'd passed disappear into the distance and never seeing what was approaching—the story of my life. If I got this job, things might be different, with new friends and a new location giving me a fresh start in life.

The horizontal pattern of the rain on the window ran erratically toward the rotund, green-suited senior opposite me. I couldn't decide whether his nose was too small or his black-rimmed spectacles too large. He shuffled through papers in a manila folder, occasionally glancing up and scrutinising some other occupant of the compartment. The gloomy world outside had turned the window into a useful mirror for the purpose of observing my fellow passengers without the risk of eye contact. It was my turn to be scrutinised so I moved my attention to the blond guy beside him.

His black tee shirt showed off his muscles as he sat upright with legs crossed. He was reading "August 1914" by Aleksandr Solzhenitsyn. Who actually reads that stuff? Maybe he was another boring English teacher like me — or a Russian spy.

Beside him, in the corner by the door to the corridor, a tall slim brunette in her late twenties also sat reading, but I couldn't see what. She was eating some kind of muesli bar and using the book to catch the bits.

She kept glancing at the girl opposite who, in contrast to the others, was an unconventional looking teenager, partly hidden behind curtains of coloured hair. I couldn't help thinking how the piercings in her lips and nose would create substantial intimacy problems with a partner having a similar taste in fashion — especially if the various metal rings acquired some residual magnetism. With ears plugged into another world, listening to her tinned music, her thumbs were a blur, texting, tweeting or twittering. She could easily have been a student in one of my classes.

Train compartments are fertile country for a self-confessed people watcher like me. Sometimes someone would start up a conversation and everyone would join in, but this one was quiet as a urologist's waiting room. I glanced again at the colourful thing curled up at the end of the bench seat. I wondered how her thumbs could be so talkative and whether her tongue, pierced or otherwise, was capable of the same dexterity.

My thoughts were interrupted when the green-suited chap opposite me leant forward, glared at the girl and demanded, "Can you not see how ridiculous you look with your coloured hair and all those rings through your lips and nose?"

The hairs on the back of my neck stood up to get a better view. The blond guy glanced at the green suit and then at the girl. The tall lady stopped halfway through a bite while her eyes flitted around the compartment.

The target of this venom continued breathing normally. Calmly pulling the earpiece from her left ear and looking at the green suit with an expression of mild irritation, she replied, "Do you realise you're wearing odd socks?"

Recoiling from this counter attack and glancing toward his feet, "Rubbish!" he scoffed. "They both match, they're both blue!"

With a patronising smile, she quietly continued.

"Green suit, loud orange tie, blue socks? They look pretty odd to me, but *I* wouldn't be so rude as to describe you as ridiculous even if you *are* devoid of any sense of style."

"How dare you speak to me in that manner!" he snorted.

"I may well ask you the same question Sir, and I'll thank you to keep your small-minded opinions to yourself," she replied. Turning away toward the corridor window and in a much quieter voice she added, "Go tickle your ass with a feather."

"What did you say?" exploded the green-suit.

Giving him a steely gaze she leant toward him, using a much louder voice, "I said it's particularly nasty weather."

She then sat back in her seat in a relaxed manner and replaced her dangling ear-piece. A quick glance at the other two told me that all three of us were sitting in a dense atmosphere of suppressed mirth. It was the most unexpected exchange I have ever encountered. I was well practised in the art of keeping a straight stern face to control a class, but this was too much. I tried, with limited success, to hide a wide grin behind my hand. The tall lady stood up, hastily brushed crumbs from her dress and left—I assumed, to have a loud belly-laugh while rolling around outside in the corridor. The young chap beside the green suit was more restrained and focussed on pulling a loose thread from the bottom of his tee shirt.

"What are you laughing at?" the green-suit barked at me in a sergeant major tone. Contrary to the intention, this made it even more comical and I blurted out, "I'm sorry, but that was the funniest thing I've ever heard."

The suit leapt to his feet. "Funny? You think it's funny?" he shouted.

I'm sure he would have continued but the young blond guy beside him also stood and put a gentle hand on his shoulder. "Okay, my friend," he said, still smiling, "it's time to take a deep breath. I need you to calm yourself and sit down. Now."

As they both resumed their seats the door slid open to reveal a very serious looking ticket inspector.

"Is there a problem in here?" he asked sternly.

The young guy eyeballed the green-suit and repeated the question.

Glancing around the compartment from the edge of his seat, the green-suit seemed to recognise the balancing point of the situation and slowly sank back as we awaited his answer.

"No problem here," he replied in a thin voice.

The blond guy looked across to me, "Does anyone else have a problem?"

I sensed that the temperature had dropped dramatically and that the blond guy's personality was dominant.

"No problem," I replied, turning to look at the young girl beside me.

She was calm and composed.

"No problem here," she said with a surprised inflexion.

"That's good to hear," said the inspector as he backed out of the doorway.

The brunette, discretely observing from the safety of the corridor, cautiously returned and sat again in the corner. There was a tense silence, eventually broken by the teenager.

She stood up and said, "Ladies and gentlemen, my name is Jessica Theodopolous. I would like to introduce you to my grumpy grandfather in the corner Mr Sol Theodopolous.'

A deluge of questions poured through my mind as I waited in silence, anticipating some kind of nuclear explosion, but Mr Theodopolous smiled amiably and did a common wave to all. His demeanour was totally different and I wondered if perhaps he had secretly taken a sensible-pill.

Jessica said that she would like her grandfather to say a few words.

This should be good, I thought.

He shuffled to the edge of his seat to be able to clearly see all of us and said in a quite normal tone, "Thank you for your attention." Looking along the seat on his side of the compartment, he said, "Michael, Joanne," and then at me, "Margaret."

His Orwellian knowledge of my name bounced even more questions around in my head.

"First I must apologise for my outburst and for

the deception," he continued. "You are undoubtedly wondering how I know your names. You'll be surprised to find that I know a lot more about you and your reasons for being on this train. Joanne, you are travelling to Sydney for an interview at the Susan Grayson private school for the position of senior English teacher."

The blond guy visibly jumped, looking alternately between us. My heart jumped because this was the position I was travelling to Sydney for.

"Yes, the three of you are all candidates for the same position. So how do I know this?"

He held our undivided attention.

"The school very generously organised your travel arrangements so it was possible to book us all into the same compartment. I have been engaged by the school to provide personality assessments, prior to your final interviews later today. The assessment involves observing how you react to potentially stressful and confrontational, real-life situations. We specialise in creating the conditions required to do such a test. The assessment has now been completed. Before submitting a written report, we are required to ask if you have any objection to it being used by the school."

I was suffering from an overdose of mixed feelings. I felt annoyed at this oblique approach but I was also keen to get this job. Should I revel in the satisfaction of slapping him around the head? If I did, would it be viewed as a good thing or a bad thing? I was sorely tempted to say stick the job, but perhaps this was also part of the test, to sort out who would react how? Would it be a black mark to accept the test, showing a propensity to take the easiest solution? I hated psych tests because I never knew which way an answer would be viewed. I felt that I'd behaved in an appropriate manner in the face of his little tirade. What should I do? The other two were clearly wrestling with similar thoughts. There was a limit to how long the pregnant silence would be acceptable. It didn't look like anyone else was about to respond so I decided there would be merit points in taking the initiative.

"I have to say that I am now questioning whether I even want to work at a school that engages in such underhanded methods." I was aware of the other two nodding in agreement. "However, I boarded this train because I am seriously interested in this position, so my answer must be yes. I will agree with the assessment being used, but I will also be discussing the method and the manner with the school at the appropriate time."

Mr Theodopolus smiled. "Thank you, Margaret. What about you Michael?"

"Margaret sums up my feelings perfectly."

Sol Theodopolus looked rather smug. He moved his attention to Joanne who sat in deep thought, supporting her head with both hands. She was also trembling lightly.

"And you, Joanne?" he asked.

Without a word, she stood and carefully retrieved her briefcase from the overhead rack. "You'll be disappointed to hear that I'm not of the same mind," she said while opening the case. She pulled out a small black wallet and opened it up for Mr Theodopolous to see.

"I am Detective Inspector Joanne Watts and I am arresting you for public nuisance, threatening behaviour and for being a thoroughly despicable person. We've received a number of complaints about you and have been watching you for some time. I am obliged to warn you that anything you say may be written down and used in evidence against you." Everyone watched in silence as she flipped open her mobile and rang a number. "Sergeant, I've just made the arrest. Have a paddy wagon at the station, please. Yes, it's all on video," she said, glancing up at her bag in the overhead rack. "We've got everything... No, if he gives me any trouble I'll Taser the bastard... Yeh, hopefully. I haven't used the new D12 Taser yet. Tell the team 'mission accomplished'. Good work everyone. See you when we arrive. Bye."

Jessica, looking decidedly less composed, probably wanted to press an undo button, or switch something off. Sol Theodopolous already looked stunned *without* the use of a Taser.

"Look, we didn't mean to upset anyone," he

pleaded. "It's just the method that we use."

"Shut it!" snapped Joanne, stabbing a finger at the man. "Save it for the judge. I've got my methods too. I'm looking forward to having a chat with you in the intimate ambience of the interrogation room. I'll need you two as witnesses," she said, glancing at Michael and I. "It would be useful if one or both of you could make a formal complaint. It will allow us to take blood and urine samples — and do a cavity search."

I'm sure it was this final indignity that caused Mr Theodopolous to slump back in a dead faint.

"Oh crap!" said Joanne. "That wasn't supposed to happen. I might have pushed it a bit too far. Jessica, quick! Go and get the ticket inspector. Tell him to bring a first aid kit and oxygen."

Jessica hesitated, appearing unsure whether to stay with her grandfather or to obey Joanne's commands. With an ashen face, she decided to comply with a police directive.

Michael had loosened the loud orange tie and undone the top button of his patient's shirt. He was patting the ghostly white face and I could see signs of a response.

"Can I do anything?" I asked.

"Not really," replied Joanne. "Serves the silly old fool right for pulling such a stupid trick."

"Do you think he'll go to prison?" I asked.

"No, but I might," replied Joanne, searching for further signs of recovery.

"What do you mean?" I asked.

With a wry grin, she explained. "I bought the police badge from eBay… in case someone tried to mug me. I just thought the smug little bastard should have a taste of his own medicine."

MONSTER

Fiona Emily

The acrid stench makes her eyes water. She breathes through her mouth; anything to avoid the taste of tainted air that has her thinking about decomposing flesh. There are more pressing matters to focus on, like the fact she has no clue where she is or how she got here. But it's hard to ignore the foul smell. Especially when it's so close, lingering over her collapsed form, like it's waiting to devour her.

Darkness makes every shadow more ominous. She recognises nothing, seeing indistinct shapes as she glances about. There is ground beneath her. Gravel has scratched itself into her palms. High in the sky are the moon and stars.

She shifts. Rising to a crouch, her joints stretch.

There's a soreness that wasn't there before but she can't remember why or how. But that smell… the stench carries with it a memory that tastes too much like fear.

The throbbing in her head makes it difficult to discern any flashes of memory. All she has are her senses and a deep foreboding that grows with every passing second.

A noise in the silence sends her heartbeat into a flurry. Every muscle tightens as she listens intently, hoping that crunch in the earth nearby was part of her imagination.

A scattering of stones starts a trembling within her. Vibrations in the ground follow, that speaks of something sizable. And close. She crinkles her nose at the invading smell, growing worse with every breath.

She holds still, waiting, praying the darkness will be her shield. That she might be safe, despite the panic clawing its way up her throat. She looks to the stars, seeking their guidance. Except there are no stars visible. They're lost, blocked out by a large black mass that fills the sky.

She springs forward, scrambling to her feet. A burst of hot sour air hits the back of her neck like it wishes to consume her. Desperation has her clawing at the dirt, searching for grip to propel her faster, anything to get away.

She finds some semblance of balance and pushes off, rocks stabbing her bare feet. Behind her, in between scattered urgent breaths, she hears hulking steps chasing her down.

She runs as fast as she can, thrashing her way past trees, with no time to dodge swiping branches that slow her escape.

A burst of charged air fans her neck. She blinks quickly and before she can put on a burst of speed, she's hit from behind. The force drives her whole body forward, crashing to the ground. A dark shadow materialises above her.

The blackness consumes her. A scream erupts from her throat as sharp talons crush her face into the dirt.

Light drowns her eyes. She blinks slowly, the panic difficult to wade through. With the light on, the blanketing haze dwindles. The familiar comes into view - the small teddy lamp now alight in the corner. Pink walls covered with boy band posters. The soft covers of her heart bedspread clenched tightly between her fingers.

See? There are no monsters.

A figure sits in the brown varnished chair beside her bed. She is watched by blue eyes, eyes she knows, eyes so much like her own.

"Dad?"

He must have heard her screams and come to help her fight off her darkness. Never has she felt more grateful to see him. She takes a long slow breath, hoping it might still the pounding of her heart.

He reaches out to touch her arm. Lines wrinkle his forehead. She is certain from his expression that he knows what it's like to have dreams plagued by darkness and fear. His touch is a welcome comfort. This man she loves will protect her from whatever may chase her in the dark haze of a dream.

Exhaling heavily she scans the room one more time, fighting off the unease. It was just a dream. The shadows, the darkness they were wrong.

There is no monster.

Hands still shaking, she sits up. Her toes languish in the soft rug on the floor, but it's not enough to quell her fears. She closes the gap to her father, seeking the warmth of a hug.

He pulls her into his arms, wrapping her up tightly. She tucks her face into his chest and breathes in the scent of his familiar aftershave.

"It's okay. I'll always be with you," he whispers quietly into her tangled hair. In his arms, the tension lessens and little by little, her racing heart rate slows. She feels calm when he lifts up and lowers her back onto the bed.

He sits beside her, the bed dipping under his weight. Head resting on her soft pillow, she looks up at him. He watches her intently, a silent tear tracking down his face.

He's sad. Why is he sad? Come to think of it, when was the last time she witnessed the full bloom of happiness on his face?

She smiles up at him, hoping the gesture might

bring the same respite he brought her, wanting desperately to chase away the lingering sadness within him.

"I love you, Dad," she whispers quietly.

His hand reaches out to skim her cheek. Palm open, his fingers spread out over her upturned lips like her smile is something he can't bear to see.

Her mouth lifts wider, certain if she smiles enough for them both, it might overcome what burdens him.

Breathing heavily, he leans in. "I love you, my little bunny," he chokes out as he presses a feather-light kiss to her forehead.

She sees his anguish as he draws away from her, tears now streaking down his face.

What's wrong?

But there's no room to ask because his hand clamps down on her lips.

The pale lamplight is blocked by the dark form hovering over her. The puff of air she manages to suck through heavy fingers smells pungent, a mixture of sweat and bile that makes her stomach turn violently. Her heart slams against her chest, panic an unwelcome visitor.

She searches for words but there's no space for them. There's barely room to breathe with his fingers digging into the flesh of her cheeks. But she's not giving up. She searches the face of her father, desperate for him to see the hope in her eyes, pleading with him to make a different choice.

His eyes meet hers for a fleeting second. There's a flicker of sorrow before darkness clouds them.

His response is to squeeze his eyes shut.

The pressure on her face increases, engulfing her mouth and nose. She thrashes about and screams out to him, but it can't be heard. Her chest wheezes for air but there is none to be found. She tries to shift, to wriggle free, she kicks and bucks, but the weight upon her is an unshiftable force.

The hand that grips her face feels like a talon, the cutting pressure deep and painful. Tears well in her eyes; the last of her silent pleas.

She blinks away the blurriness, clinging with all she has left, to the familiar. The smooth skin of her father's face, his dark curls now tinged with grey, the comfort of his open arms.

As darkness closes in, as the last puff of air recedes from her lungs, four words echo in her mind.

He is no monster.

He is no monster.

POPPIES IN THE SUNLIGHT

Sophie L. Macdonald

Have you ever thought about how you want to die? I have. I want it to be on an ordinary day. No last cruise or a trip on the Orient Express. I want to have breakfast, lunch, dinner, and a cup of tea before bed. I want my husband to walk in the following morning, clutching a fistful of poppies that he's just picked from the garden, and find me lying there—beautiful in my best pink satin nightgown—and drop to his knees with sorrow, poppies sprinkled around him on the carpet like bright drops of blood in the morning sun.

"Helen!" he'll exclaim, doubled over with grief. "Helen! Don't you understand that I just can't live without you?"

I'm not sure what happens at that point. Perhaps

he grabs the nearest bottle of Valium (and there are always plenty of those in our house) and, like Romeo, throws the contents down his throat until the need to sleep overcomes him, and he dies by my side. Is there an afterlife? Maybe we meet up on a cloud somewhere, and I've changed into my white trouser suit that makes me look a bit like a Heavenly Hillary Clinton, and we eat canapés and laugh about it all.

"Gosh Derek," I'll drawl languidly, as I imagine that is how I will speak when I'm in Heaven. For some reason, I also hear myself talking with an American accent, but I'm not sure why. "That was so bourgeois of you. Randy at the golf club will never be able to top you topping yourself!" Then we will both throw back our heads and laugh, as my hair cascades down my back like it never did when I was alive. I don't know who Randy is, either, but it strikes me that he'd be the kind of guy that imaginary American us are always competing with.

"Randy's gone and bought a new Land Rover, damn it," Derek would say whilst we were still alive (in my imaginary parallel universe, of course). I would look up from baking biscuits—I mean cookies—and smile angelically.

"He can have as many cars as he likes, but he won't have what we have," I'll say in a twinkly voice. And then Derek would come closer and kiss me, and the smell of cookies would fill the air.

I have a lot of fantasies about our life as a perfect American couple. Maybe when I die—when we die—some of those fantasies will come true. Who knows what kind of afterlife is out there anyway?

Sometimes she sneaks into the dream, and I have to remember that I am in control and I can stop it whenever I like. We'll be sat there on our cloud (dead and American, of course), and Derek will suddenly look at something over my shoulder. I'll crane around trying to see what he's looking at, and then I see her. She's not even dressed for the occasion—just wearing the same old jeans and t-shirt that she always wears. I've seen her at the shops before, and she thinks I don't know who she is, but I know. Her, in her jeans and t-shirt, looking for all the world like a regular person. I see her.

Then Derek, still on his cloud, pretends he was just looking around Heaven. He leans closer and brushes a strand of hair out of my eyes. It wasn't even in my eyes. I don't want him to touch me. I want him to fall through his cloud and never come back, and I want thunder and lightning to fire to consume the heavens, and for the last thing I see to be her anguished, pained face. It can turn into Hell if I get to see her burn.

And then I realise that I'm sitting at the kitchen table, clutching my whisky a little too hard and the glass is empty all over again. Sometimes I can't even make the dream happen again, and I just have to take my Valium and go to sleep for real. I never have actual dreams—just the ones I control.

I remember when I first saw her. Derek told me some hard luck story about an annoying receptionist at work. She was a single mum, her car had broken down and he had to give her a lift home. I had nothing else to do so I went, and I watched, and I saw them leave together. Then I went home as fast as I could, and I waited to make sure he was back at his normal time. He was. And most people would have thought nothing was out of the ordinary at all, but I saw it. A light behind his eyes that used to be there a very long time ago.

You might wonder why dead American dream Derek and Helen don't have any dead American dream children. The stupid thing is that I tried. I tried to picture them. A boy and a girl, maybe, or twin girls. They could be sitting on their own clouds, and playing with toys or whatever children do but, the thing is, I can see the cloud really clearly, but I can't see the children. So unimaginative, Helen. I failed to produce children in real life, so it shouldn't surprise me that I can't whip some up in a fantasy afterlife either.

She has a boy. I saw him run out to meet her on one occasion when Derek dropped her home. Derek got out of the car to greet him, and it struck me that anyone looking on would think they were the real family. Derek was so interested in him— crouching down and throwing a ball to him. Then he went inside. Just went inside the house. I didn't know what to do, so I drove home. Derek came home hours later and told me that he had gone for drinks with the boys from work. He even used those words, which sounded almost comical coming from him. Derek didn't drink. He didn't even like my drinking, although I don't drink that much and it's only because I have nothing else to do.

Derek phoned me this afternoon to say that he would be late home tonight—really late. The boys (who, by the way, I have no idea are, as he mostly works with a collection of middle aged ladies and a twenty-year-old student) were having a night out, and I would be in bed before he got back. He told me not to wait up, and that it would probably be morning before I saw him. I didn't say anything for a while, and he probably thought I was upset. I wasn't. I knew where he would be, and I've grown quite used to it. I guess he must enjoy playing families with her. There was a really long silence and he asked me if I'd been drinking. I said no. We both knew that wasn't true. He asked if he could bring anything home, and one thing occurred to me, so I told him. He seemed surprised but agreed. I think he just wanted to get me off the phone.

I'm waiting for him now, but I think I'll be asleep before he gets here. I'm getting nervous that I forgot something, but I think it's all in place. I reposition myself on the bed. The pink nightgown doesn't fit as well as I thought it did, but I think it will look okay if I keep lying on my back. I try to look down at my tummy, but everything is sliding out of focus. I hope Derek remembers the poppies.

SCHOOL

Lorraine A. Slim

Answers, questions, symbols and equations filter into the dark. I scramble to see the time, 1:30 AM…

I startle awake and throw mangled covers off my sweat slick body. My pyjamas are soaked and hair clings to my cheeks. Kneading my tense forehead, I drag my legs over the side of the bed.

Why has nobody woken me?

I focus on the clock digits. It's only 5:00 AM. Sitting for a moment, I contemplate whether to get up or try to grab more sleep. So many hours with so little rest since I first checked the time. A workload is due today that I haven't managed to complete. I am haunted by the noise, stress, and inevitable abuse that every day offers. I choose not to torture myself further and struggle to stand upright.

The shower is long, cool and refreshing but it can't refresh a tired mind. I brush my long strands and leave them wet to drip like tears hiding my real ones. The bathroom is bright and clean as the sun streaks through the blinds onto shiny white tiles; they are cool and offer comfort at the start of my day. An urge not to leave fills my body and I sit on the cold floor with my arms wrapped about me holding in the pain. The day is going to reach 38°C with humidity plus, but I have to get to school.

I dress in mandatory shirt and skirt but leave my feet bare as I wander through to the kitchen. Juice, toast and fruit are forced down my throat and I gag with thoughts of that place.

I don't want to go.

Expectations at school are high and I stare at textbooks in front of me. So much to do.

"Must carry on, must get this done," I say, trying to find a little motivation.

I open the first book and pick up a pen. It seems impossible in the time I have and my head buzzes. Painkillers just don't work anymore but I take a couple anyway.

Distraction is easy with texts and social media. I jab a comment as a reply to a friend's post.

"I must push through this," I mutter.

With lunch packed, I head out of the house with a full bag and an empty heart. The trip to school fills with thoughts of what might occur today: bullies, bad attitudes and brain ache. I have the rest of my work to do during first break and a tuition session on second break.

Entering the school grounds, my hollow heart aches and I freeze on the threshold.

Point of no return. I take a long breath and hold it in for a moment. *Here goes.*

I plant a small smile on my lips and nod to the occasional friendly face as my heart sets a faster beat. The principal's face is more deeply grooved than usual as he looks at his watch and then at me. "Don't you have a class to be at?"

My smile doesn't falter whilst my pace quickens to the rhythm in my chest and I give him a frantic, stupid set of nods.

Entering the final class of the day, I long for today to be over. Late as usual, I walk into chaos. Screwed up paper flies across the room. Max the class idiot - or should I say the worst of the idiots - is standing on my desk. I stare at him in disbelief like it hasn't happened before. His look is one of defiance as he carries on attempting hip hop to a beat emanating from his girlfriend's phone, who is too busy twerking to notice my presence. Bile and a hurried lunch grabs at my throat. The books in my hands spill to the floor. My heart burns with speed and my hands ball into fists as I attempt to control my anger.

"Master Gyrating Jacobs! Please remove yourself from my desk and report to the Behavioural Unit immediately. Miss Twerky Taylor, give me that phone. Your parents will be required to pick this up from the office. And the rest of you, sit down and shut up!"

The kids move at my command and Billy retrieves the textbooks from the floor and places them in a neat pile on my desk. Max Jacobs gyrates out of the door and Zina Taylor hands her phone over with a mouthed, "Sorry Miss" and silly grin. She swiftly takes her place amongst her silenced classmates.

"I have the results of last week's test and, for the record, most of you did quite well, including you Zina." I give her a nod and smile as I hand her test paper back. She spots the A minus and beams broadly.

"Thank you, Miss," she gushes whilst hiding her smile from the rest of the class.

"And thank you," I return.

It's the first A in Maths for this average student. The extra tuition at lunchtimes has made a difference and my heart warms at her gratitude.

THE CLEANER

R. A. Purtill

Above the awkward silence in the facilities at the Cineplex where I waited for the cubicle, I heard the sound of scratching and squeaking and smelled the sharp odour of a marking pen.

When the sound stopped and the door opened, the occupant pushed past me, his head low and covered in a hoodie. He didn't stop to wash his hands and in his haste to leave, bumped into my cleaning trolley. It clattered to the floor and threw out its contents of bottles, rags, buckets and brooms. In his chaotic departure, he dropped something. It was caught under the front wheel. I corrected the trolley, gathered the gear and picked up the wallet. It fell open in my hand. Despite its personal nature, or perhaps because of it, I was reluctant to close it. It might provide a clue to the stranger. It didn't. There was a photo of a girl grinning from behind her wild, blonde hair. The life in her eyes caused my heart to skip but I didn't know her. A scrap of paper dropped out. It had an address on it but that didn't mean anything either. I put it back together, shoved it in my pocket and, with a mental reminder about lost property, continued to clean. I squeezed into the cubicle.

There on the back of the door in big, black angular letters were the words GOD FORGIVE ME. My own big, black angular letters!

Max called out then so I was released from the shock that had begun to do its work on my knees.

"You done yet, Andy?"

"Get in here."

"What? No."

"Just come look at this."

Max put his head round the door and glanced at the graffiti. "So, clean it off and let's get out of here."

But I was fixed on those words. "Does this writing look familiar to you?"

Max sighed and we swapped places, sliding by each other through the door.

"So, it's yours. Is this some kind of joke?" He pushed his way out again. "What are you trying to do, make work for yourself?"

"Did you see a guy rush out of here?"

"No. I just got out of six." Cinema number six

was on the other side of the Cineplex; he couldn't have seen anything. I was in a cold sweat and moisture left my mouth. I took out the wallet with trembling hands.

"Are you alright?" he asked.

I handed him the photo.

"Nice." He turned it over. "Louise," he read. Then his mouth opened wide. "2022? You expect me to believe this is from the future?" He scoffed and threw it back. "Come on. We'll miss the last bus."

I followed him out pushing the trolley. "I think I just met my future self, man."

"There's no such thing as time travel because it causes rips in the time-space continuum and entropic cascade failure and it tears the universe apart and then..." he paused, his face close, "... it blows your mind." He pushed his index finger into my forehead.

In that instant, the sound of repeated gunfire echoed from the street and the glass door at the entrance exploded. I dove behind the trolley while Max raced to the source of the noise. He soon returned to squat with me behind our metal bunker.

"There's someone lying just outside. Shot. Looks like Eric Sanderson."

"The drug pusher?"

"Is he?"

"Good."

Max stared at me. "What?"

"It's about time someone…" How many times had I thought of doing just that?

The noises in the street rose. Sirens, alarms and shouts of 'Someone's been shot' and 'Call the police.'

We decided it was safe to move out and as we did, the dude from the bathroom staggered into the shattered foyer, without his hoodie, I noticed. He grabbed Max by the collar. 'I shot him. I did it.' But then he looked across at me with panic on his face. MY FACE!

"No," he cried and dragged Max with him into the men's room. I was going to follow but my head was spinning and my stomach lurched. I held the trolley until the rush subsided and then I joined them.

Max was kneeling over my doppelgänger who was rolling in pain and vomiting on the tiles I had just cleaned.

"Save her," he said between sobs.

"The wallet, quick." Max put out his hand toward me.

When I hesitated, he said, "It's okay, you'll get it back." I handed it over.

"Save Louise." The guy stabbed at the picture with a bloodied finger.

"Is he bleeding?" I asked.

"No. It must be Eric's, but he seems to be having a heart attack."

Max folded the guy's hand around the wallet and pressed it into his heaving chest.

"Can't meet myself… get him out." He started convulsing.

"I'm not going anywhere." I grabbed the sink as much to make my point as for support when the nausea started again.

"Ask him what happens," I said through the rising bile.

"They destroy her. Don't let the drugs destroy her." He was looking at Max but I knew he was speaking to me.

And then my head exploded with the insanity of being in the same space as my future self and with the burden of some responsibility I did not understand.

When the pounding stopped, I knew what I had to do. My reflection in the clean mirror affirmed my next move. It was going to hurt. I let go of the sink and dropped to the floor beside them.

"Why did you come?" I grabbed the other guy's shirt with both hands as our worlds collided.

"For Louise."

"No. Why here, when you knew the chances of meeting?" My arms were paralysed and the strength in my hands melted away. I dropped him back to the floor.

"It's where the portal is… no choice." He rolled to his side away from me.

No choice. While our timelines diverged forever

from that point, I knew we were the same. No choice. I forced myself through the pain and put my hand on his shoulder until his legs curled up into his chest and he gasped.

"Louise. I'm sorry."

The air around him warped and folded in on itself. He let out a final scream that echoed around the room and vibrated through me as he vanished.

Silence has never been part of our friendship but now together on the bathroom floor, Max and I sat in our own quiet, internal spaces. When he stood again and gestured for me to do the same, broken timelines reconnected.

"Looks like it's over. Come on." He helped me to stand. "Who's Louise?"

All I could do was stare at the floor. All signs of the guy's chunder had vanished. The clean tiles conspired to cover a future I would now deny.

In the foyer, a policeman was running tape around the broken window and across the floor. He stopped and looked at us. "You work here?"

We nodded.

"You'll have to come to the station with me." He tied off the tape and directed us to the car parked outside. "This way."

Out in the street, ambulance officers hoisted a gurney into the back of their van. When they drove away, the lingering crowd drifted in various directions up and down the street.

Max slid into the patrol car first, so I was in the

middle when a crumpled mess of a girl flopped in beside me.

Our eyes met and a new path was forged.

As we pulled away from the kerb, Max thumped me. "From the photo," he mouthed, "that's her."

"I know," I replied, rubbing my shoulder.

She turned from the window and said, "You're Andy?" When I nodded stupidly, she pushed the hoodie at me. "Then that's yours." I looked down at the future thing lying in my lap.

"The wallet. I never got the wallet back." I said to Max.

The girl smiled then, her eyes bright.

"You have to wait for your birthday. I give it to you then."

THE JOB

Jodie Lane

It was the hardest job she'd ever done. The hours were ridiculous; shift work like you wouldn't believe! And the breaks — what breaks? Surely there were laws about that? But it wasn't as if she was on any kind of award wage. Conditions that would have any Fair Work official objecting were completely ignored in this industry. Sure, there was no uniform and she didn't have to travel far, but the negative aspects far outweighed the positive ones in this instance.

And her boss. Well, he was the real reason this job was so hard. Poor communicator? Tick. Extremely emotional? Tick. Yells, screams, changes his mind? Tick! Tick! Tick!

But there was no point saying it wasn't fair. 'If

you didn't want this job, why did you quit your old one?' people would ask. Ooh, her old boss would surely love to see her come crawling back, to say she couldn't hack it. Well, she wouldn't give them the satisfaction! She'd take the abuse and the shitty hours and just suck it up. Push through it. Surely once she got the hang of things it would get easier? As long as she didn't kill herself or her boss in the meantime...

"How's things?" people wanted to know.

"Oh, you know." She'd smile brightly and drown her voice in false cheer. "Getting there!"

She couldn't ask for help. Too much pride. Too much pressure. Had to be seen to be succeeding. Keep on top of things. Otherwise, people would think she was a failure. She'd know she was a failure.

Keep smiling, keep performing. "Oh, you are doing a good job!" they would say. "It's hard, but obviously you are managing well!" They didn't see the tears. The frustration. They didn't know how she dreaded waking up each morning, unable to face another endless day at work. She'd crawl into bed and dream of it, or worse, lie awake thinking of it, knowing she needed her rest but unable to do so, then hating herself even more for it.

The hate. That was it. She hated herself for taking this job. She hated her boss. But she couldn't say that. Oh no. That wasn't allowed. Instead, it ate up inside of her, poisoning the times when her boss was in a good mood or not hassling her. She was on edge all the time, waiting for the next crisis, the next demand. She couldn't enjoy her time off, even when she got away from work. It was all she could think about and she felt guilty that she wasn't better at her job.

Finally, it got too much. Something snapped. Her boss was screaming at her so she simply turned around and walked out of the room. Outside, into the fresh air. She felt like she hadn't seen the sun in an age.

Phone out. Dial.

"Mum?"

"Hi, honey! How are you?"

Silence.

"Honey? Are you there? Is everything okay?"

"Mum." Voice cracking. She could still hear her boss screaming inside. He was really furious this time.

"Honey, what's wrong?"

"Mum, I need help. I'm not coping. I'm scared..."

It was a lifesaving phone call. She didn't quit her job, oh no. But once she'd been diagnosed with post-natal depression, the air - while still not clear - was breathable. She didn't have to be okay. There was help, for her and her baby.

SOMETIMES LUCKY

Helen Low

Distanced from her husband by more than the cool space of linen between them in the double bed, Christina clenched her hands. Our home is our castle, she thought.

Next, he'll expect me to invite them here for dinner!

"Chrissie, why so unreasonable?" Alex, face shadowed by the company report, carefully not allowing his legs to touch hers, had read her mood exactly. But his tone was non-committal, "I suppose I could say you were called to your parents?"

"I just don't want to go!" She hoped he didn't sense her apprehension at being put under the microscope to be tried and found wanting. 'It's you they want to interview. I won't be on their payroll!'

"No?" The report fell between them, an ironic symbol of their disagreement, then it was gone, tossed to the floor. "If I get the job there'll be travel involved. I'd be entitled to take you. Wouldn't you want to come? Travelling costs money."

Does Alex resent having to provide for everyone, the school fees, the holidays? The silence of the house was interrupted, each sound distinct as the ring of a pebble tossed into a well... that was the rattle of the front door opening, then the bang as it shut. William is in, and it's 11.30. Another door... David going to the kitchen.

"The boys are at the fridge again!"

"Don't knock it, darling. If it wasn't for the fridge they wouldn't recognise each other." He saw her face, felt the pent-up fear and anger.

"Joke, Chrissie. They're growing boys. They have their own friends."

How can he be so casual? The company has taken him... soon our sons will fly the nest. A coldness ran through her at the thought of empty bedrooms, a house without boys.

"Come on, Chris! We'll have dinner with the directors and I'll book a room. It's a long time since we've had a night in a luxury hotel."

Not since our honeymoon, and that was eighteen years ago.

He stroked her hair and she turned towards him. "That's better, Chrissie. You'll be able to have a look at the shops or meet some of the girls for the afternoon and I'll join you there."

The taxi drove under the portico and the doorman opened her door. Accustomed to driving herself, she had no money ready to pay the driver and she caught up with her luggage at the desk. The exquisite blonde receptionist was no older than William. "You have a reservation, ma'am?" she asked.

"Maclaine. Mr and Mrs Alex Maclaine." She watched her as her perfectly manicured hand ran down the register. "We have no reservation under that name, ma'am," and excused herself to answer an incoming call. "Your wife is here now, Mr Maclaine." She summoned a bell-boy and gave him a key from the board and flashed a pearly smile, "Have a nice day."

Why did Alex leave it so late to phone? Why did he make a simple thing so involved?

The centre lift opened. She stood beside the bell-boy, aware of the creases in her cream linen suit, wishing her bag was smarter, while numbers raced to 26 and the mirrored doors slid open.

She followed along the corridor and he unlocked a door and stood aside... beige carpet, beige upholstery, beige curtains and an arrangement of wooden legs and leather straps at the foot of the bed. She watched him adjust its height and place her scuffed leather suitcase in its personalised cradle and recalled swaddled dolls of Christmases past and towels and crowns she had provided so the boys could take their places by the manger. Now he was watching her, waiting with a smile. An infuriating, all-knowing smile.

He thinks I'm here to further an illicit affair!

Sudden anger flared at Alex and the directors of the company who presumed the wife of a prospective executive came as part of a package deal. "My husband will be joining me later," she said briskly.

"Yes, ma'am. Will that be all?"

She pressed a note into his hand, hoping the amount was appropriate then decided as he backed toward the door that she really didn't care.

Behind one pair of limed-oak louvre doors was a wardrobe with plastic coat-hangers attached to a rail. She started to hang up her clothes, hanging the pleated black georgette skirt and the turquoise pin-tucked shirt so the creases would fall, and placed her unremarkable black suede pumps on the shoe rack underneath.

The best aspect of the room was the view. She drew at white cords until the curtains were contained in neat pleats and stood watching racing yachts, a ferry crossing to Manly and a liner being tugged out to the Heads.

She guessed at its ports of call and imagined liaisons occasioned by romantic moonlit evenings, then flushed at the memory of the bellboy's fleeting smile and her gauche apology for having arrived alone.

Why did Alex accede to this charade? Of what possible interest to Alex's prospective employers was Christina Maclaine, whom a quirk of fate had made his wife?

She could have married Sam and lived in New York in a penthouse overlooking Park Avenue. She might have married Geoffrey, who at the latest account was excavating some new dig in northern Greece.

Her suit was crushed but that was the nature of the fabric. She undressed, hanging the skirt and jacket beside her evening wear in the wardrobe and turned on the taps in the shower.

Alex might have married Sandra, and damn near did. But Sandra had dropped him, bewitched by Roger, a suave medical student with a sporty, blue MG. Sometimes you can be lucky, she thought. Sometimes you can be very, very lucky.

Had Alex ever understood her insecurity at having caught him on the rebound? The needles of water stung her body and she stood until she was filled with pleasant lethargy, then let the water run warm. She hadn't brought her fur or an evening jacket because they were dining downstairs. Damn-she should have taken more time selecting her dinner dress, perhaps bought something new. But the boys' school fees had to be paid, and Alex's subscription to the golf club.

She had arrived too early, giving herself an

afternoon to think of things which could go wrong. She shrugged into a white terry robe from the pair folded on the tiled surround of the hand basin and towelled her hair.

Panelling beside the wardrobe disclosed cupboards and a small refrigerator. She took a fluted goblet and a half-bottle of Lanson, deciding there were occasions when one could drink alone...

She took the glass to the window. The tug was returning to the wharf and the liner had passed from sight. The racing yachts were off Pinchgut, luffing into the breeze.

She adjusted the unfamiliar controls of the dryer until warm air blew her hair dry enough to brush into its familiar style, then took nail polish from the pink cosmetic bag and applied the first coat, then another, while the yachts crisscrossed to Rushcutters Bay. Pouring the last of the champagne, she considered how to spend the afternoon until Alex arrived at six.

The worst of the creases had fallen out of her suit and she dressed leisurely, having still not made up her mind. As she closed the door behind her a phone began to ring, a muted sound that might have come from any of the rooms, so she continued on her way.

There was a vacant banquette beside a column supporting an exotic arrangement of foliage and flowers and she slipped his note from the envelope: 'Keep happy, darling. Detained until 7.30'

Even while I wait in this ridiculously expensive hotel, Alex's work comes first!'

Barely able to conceal the surging emotions she wandered past a hallway, then followed a passage blindly into a mirrored foyer lined with shops and found herself in a glamorous boutique where a gown of leopard-patterned chiffon spread across a Louis XV chair. A svelte assistant appeared through the greenery, past model gowns protected by glass cases. "Are you looking for something special?" She shook her head, "Just looking."

Christina Maclaine looks like a woman who needs something special, while some women wear these clothes every day!

An urgent need had to be assuaged, "May I try it on?"

The silk chiffon moulded her body to the waist, then flowed to her ankles in a sinuous sweep. She ran her fingers through her hair and knew herself transformed. Hardly daring to hope, she found the swing tag, flinching at the four figures, neat in calligraphic script.

Regretfully she permitted the zip to be undone. "No. Thank you," she said. "There's nothing else."

Out in the foyer, the magic of the gown remained and finding a hat-shop she had no hesitation in going inside. Recklessly she pointed to the cream straw Breton, isolated in the velvet-lined window, and took out her chequebook. Even the carry bag that came with her purchase was elegant and distinctive.

The hotel room seemed almost homely when she returned at half-past six. For the first time, she appreciated the Oriental lamps on either side of the bed and the delicacy of the Eastern figures marching steadily across the simple bridge in the screen above the headboard: men resolutely going to work in the fields. She pulled the curtains closed and turned on the lamps. Their peach-coloured shades bathed the room in warm light and the line of figures seemed imbued with a mystical symbolism. For centuries, men had gone to work to provide for the ones they loved.

With a startling clarity that shocked her, she saw herself and Alex with new eyes... a fortunate woman with a loving, responsible husband, and knew she must answer for her own dissatisfaction. If she felt discontent, it was not for opportunities lost to her by her marriage, as she had supposed, but for the choices she had made.

She could have fought for the independence of a career if she'd really wanted it and combined the two roles as many of her friends had done,- as less fortunate women were forced to do.

Alex would not have denied her the opportunity. He had even suggested they find a housekeeper if she wanted to teach when the boys went to school. Thoughtfully, she smoothed on smoke-grey stockings and then the black slip. She was putting on her makeup when his key turned in the door. He came to her eagerly, "Did you have a good day?"

She was noncommittal. "It was fine."

She hoped, as she thanked them for their hospitality, that she had said the right things, done nothing that would detract from her expression of the very model of an executive wife. As the lift rose her husband's arm was around her waist, "Chrissie, you won't be disappointed if they choose someone else?" His lips brushed her cheek then found hers.

Only for you Alex, when you want it so much...

She had fallen in love when he didn't have money and she was a newly fledged teacher and all they had was a dream. Now they were the parents of two sons and had created a home which from now on she was determined would be happy. Her voice was firm with conviction which came from her heart, "I'm sure they won't."

His jacket landed on the bed and she automatically smoothed it and took it to the wardrobe while he unknotted his tie. His face was inscrutable as he slid the silk from the confining collar of his shirt, unexpectedly vulnerable.

"I'm hoping you're right. We'd have some time together. There'd be no more golf. Someone else would have to hustle."

Secure in his arms she wondered how she could have been so wrong about so many things…

A gown had restored her sense of being a woman, but a chance meeting with Sandra had shown her expensive clothes did not ensure content.

"I ran into Roger this afternoon." Alex's voice was modulated but he was unable to veil his disapproval. "He's made a fortune and he and Sandra are off to the States. He said a change of fighting ground might stave off their divorce."

She wondered if he felt the thrill of fear run up her spine but the same calm voice continued, "Poor fool. I think he loves her. I saw her later, having a drink with one of her smart friends downstairs. Two polished, hard-faced bitches together."

Does he know me too well, or not at all? Sometimes you can be lucky. Sometimes a myopic husband can be vain enough to leave his glasses in their case.

In the morning she left the gold-lettered carry-bag at the reception desk with the beautiful girl whose smile had a warmth she had not noticed before.

"You might like this. Have a good day."
She's a nice girl. Someday she might understand…

DECIPHERING STATIC

Alicia Bruzzone

"If you think it's a ghost, how am I supposed to photograph it?" I huff as I shuffle the weight of the borrowed camera bag on my shoulder. Most people had more exciting plans on a Saturday night than breaking into deceased-estate houses. I have to assume those people have normal friends.

"I said it *might* be a ghost, Kellie. The old lady did die here," Caulder protests as he slinks up the creaky verandah stairs. "I *think* it's an alien."

This is why Caulder's stories never get printed in the school newspaper. Because journalists are supposed to presents *facts*, not the tripe he always hands in. Caulder thinks photograph evidence is all it takes to legitimise the supernatural... since there's no such thing as Photoshop.

"Did you hear that?" Caulder asks as he crouches like a cougar ready to pounce.

Radio static sparks to life from somewhere within the house, behind hushed whispers I can't decipher.

Kom heer.

My chest thumps while Caulder's face cracks into an enormous grin. "I told you, Kellie! Didn't I tell you! There's something in there."

He completes his travels up the porch in a single bound, slowly turning the creaking handle of the front door.

Wotchoo doin?

The chilling voice that calls from the depths of the gloom raises the hairs on my arm. "It's probably just a television left on somewhere," I remark to Caulder. Except it doesn't sound like a television. It barely sounds like a voice. I quickly unzip the school's camera bag and take out the camera, slipping the strap over my neck.

We work our way through the tenebrous entry, footsteps padding on worn carpet as we find the living room. It's eerily silent, our heavy breaths the only background to the awaiting room.

The static rumbles and Caulder pulls out a torch, flicking it to a lifeless TV. The beam carries over furniture to a portable radio. I flick on a side table lamp to get a better view of the equipment. My inspection falls short. It isn't even plugged in, and too light to be carrying batteries.

"It's coming from over here," Caulder whispers, the trail of light winding back out into the hall.

I shuffle after him, not wanting to be alone. I don't like the odds that someone on a tight pension had an extra television set up in a spare room, which means the noise is coming from somewhere else. Or, as much as I hate to admit it, some*thing*.

The radio static plays again, my heart bursting in time with the sudden noise.

Yu goon a eet. Ore jus look? Jus look?

I splay my palms flat against the wall as I press myself back, trying to disappear. The camera strap sticks to my clammy skin as I take a breath and regain control over my erratic fears. There is no such thing as ghosts. Or aliens. My sweaty palms indicate otherwise as I heft up the camera and chase after Caulder. "What was that?"

"Communicating long distances through space causes interference." His eyes are wide with excitement. "So it's probably an alien. The obituary did mention an unexpected death."

"She wasn't, like, mauled or anything?" I ask, wishing I'd taken Caulder's tip more seriously and actually done some research before following through with his hair-brained idea.

"Don't know," he replies cautiously, eyes strictly trained to the path of light. "I couldn't get into the funeral home to check."

He takes a step forward and the floor grunts in disapproval, echoing down the hall.

Hoose a prittie boi?

Caulder freezes, his entire body rigid as he stares at the moulded oak door to the right. The voice came from in there. And whatever it is, he's been spotted.

Wotchoo doin? Kom heer. Kom heer, the alien voice taunts.

Caulder turns paler than the ray of light that dances over the door. "They're picking up our language." He no longer sounds excited. "Kellie, get the photo and let's go!"

There's urgency in his voice as the static once more crackles down the hall, followed by a babble of language I can't decipher.

Prittie, prittie doin. Yu goon a eet, yu goon a eet. EET PRITTIE BOI.

The voice is getting louder, shrieking as it pierces the night air.

It takes me a long moment to uncap the camera, my hands sweaty and shaking. My spine chills one vertebra at a time as I force my body towards the closed door. "You'll have to reach in and turn on the light." My voice is barely audible, cracking on every syllable.

Caulder pushes the door in hesitantly, snaking a hand through the slither of opening to fumble with the wall. "On three," he mouths, colour still drained from his face.

My knees shake as I turn on the camera. Gulping down a breath, I try to force air past the lump in my throat and down into my lungs.

One.

Two.

Three.

I fling my weight at the door as Caulder flicks the light.

Hoose a prittie boi?

I fluke the focus and manage to snap a perfect picture of the old lady's pet budgerigar.

I don't think Caulder's going to make the paper.

ROSEMARY

Delia Strange

I look from my Mum, vacuuming the living room floor like she is punishing it, to my Dad, seated on the couch, his face bathed in the glow of his laptop. Through the window, the sky lingers between night and day, bathing the room in orange. I remember that moment because it is the first time she says the words, "They don't want you."

Rosemary and I often visit the playground behind my house. It's the only place I'm allowed to go unsupervised. My parents are overly protective. I understand it's because they care, but I'm old enough to look after myself. I'm almost ten.

Rosemary is sitting on one of the swings when I arrive. When she sees me, she grins and shuffles so that she stands almost straight; the seat at her bottom, her hands on the chains. Ready to start. I run to the swing beside her and mimic her position.

"Three, two, one… go!"

I lift my feet. The breeze kisses my face as I push myself higher. The best part about swinging is the magical place between forwards and backwards. It is a place where I am above the world; not rising or falling, not part of the ground or the sky. I am in my own bubble. It's a place where other kids jump off but I won't. Deep inside I know that jumping will ruin it.

We both lie on the grass and I am tickled where it touches my skin.

"That cloud looks like a rabbit," Rosemary says. I look up at a blue canvas filled with big white puffs.

"Which one?"

"The one over there, next to that little cloud on its own, see it?" She points and I look at a small cloud with a splodge of unidentifiable white beside it.

"I don't see a rabbit."

"It's sitting up."

And then I do see it; its nose is up, its ears are tucked along its body. I watched as its tail slowly detaches.

"Who are you talking to?" a boy asks. I sit up, surprised and embarrassed. I look at Rosemary, who shrugs.

"Nobody," I say, standing up.

I wipe grass off myself as the boy climbs the slide's ladder. He sits at the top and lights a cigarette, and I leave.

When the ads on the telly come on, I show my latest drawing to my dad. He takes the page and admires it. I am proud of my latest work, it has a realistic quality. I've drawn nostrils and everything.

"Is this you?" he asks and points to one of the girls in the drawing. I nod, pleased that he identified the right person. I squash onto the armchair with him.

"And who's this beside you?"

"Rosemary."

"Rosemary? Is she a friend from school?"

"Oh my God, Adam, do you not pay attention when I talk?" Mum snaps from the kitchen doorway. I unsquish myself from the chair and stand awkwardly aside. I want my drawing back but my voice is lost. Dad holds my artwork hostage as he looks at Mum.

"What?"

"Rosemary is her pretend-friend." She says it like he should know, like she's talked to him about Rosemary. I wonder what she has said but I also don't want to know.

"What, still?" Dad turns to me with creases on his brow. "Aren't you a bit old for that now?" He hands over my drawing so I can make my escape.

"Adam!" Mum says, her eyes wide and scary. As I scurry away, her eyes change to something warm and loving. "I'm sorry, darling." I shrug and continue to my room, wishing that the apology had gone to Dad instead of me. I gently close the door to block out the argument that will follow. I know Mum is trying to protect me but I don't care that Dad doesn't know who Rosemary is.

Raised voices have me turning my music on. When they get louder, Rosemary sits beside me.

"They don't want you."

"They love me," I say. My words are a meek protest to Rosemary's declaration.

"They do love you, but they don't want you."

Rosemary's words shock me into confrontation. "How does that work?"

"Because you're stopping them from getting a divorce."

I throw myself face down on the bed and curve the pillow around my ears. When I come up for air, Rosemary is gone.

Mum wants to have a week away at a cabin beside a lake. She tells me that a change of scenery might be nice. I agree with her, hoping the frantic look in her eyes will go away. I don't like seeing it on her face. Dad must not like it either because he doesn't make eye contact with her.

The brochures about the cabin show me a magical place, where smiling people on sailboats wave to laughing people picnicking on the golden shore. I imagine myself on a sailboat with Mum and Dad, the wind on my face while we race over the water. I wonder if it'll be better than the swing.

When we get there, it isn't what I expect. The cabin is tiny and smells mouldy, the beaches around the lake are stony and grey, and we aren't really by ourselves because there's a caravan park up the road filled with noisy people. Dad sets his suitcase in the middle of the room and Mum gets a look on her face that has me heading for the door.

"Darling, where are you off to?" she asks.

"The lake," I say.

"Hang on a—"

"Give her a break, she can swim," Dad interrupts Mum's cautionary words and I lunge out of the cabin before I can hear what happens next.

Rosemary walks with me down the crooked path that leads to the lake. When I get there, I see a girl my age watching a small boy build a grey sandcastle. The sky is white and flat and there are no sailboats out on the water. A couple of jet skiers are whizzing around instead, their insectile buzz annoying.

I walk up to the boy and girl, feeling the bumps of the stony sand beneath the thin soles of my sandals. The girl has curly blonde hair and she watches me approach, her hands on her hips.

"She doesn't look like a nice girl," Rosemary whispers to me on our way over.

I murmur agreement but nobody else is around so I have to try her out. The curly haired girl greets me when I draw near.

"Hi, I'm Carla, what's your name? This is my brother Brody, he has autism so he won't speak to you. He's building a trap for crabs or something, but I don't think there are any here, what do you think?"

I stare at her, my mind turning over the chunk of information that sped out of Carla's mouth. I am too slow to answer and she speaks again.

"I don't think there's any here but I won't stop him because he has to do what he has to do. I'm his big sister so I have to look out for him. It makes me very grown up, you know. Looking after little brothers or sisters does that for kids. Do you have one?"

Throughout the conversation Carla has with herself, she flips her hair and strikes poses that I've only seen the older girls at school do, so maybe she's right.

"No," I say before she can wash me in words again. My answer lights up her face in an unexpected way and she reaches out to grab my hand. My fingers twitch but I let her hold it, feeling both uncomfortable and happy.

"I'm so glad you're here, I thought I'd have to hang around a bunch of little kids all day. Not that I mind looking after my brother, because that makes me grown up, you know? But there are lots of little kids at the caravan park and nobody mature like me or you. Probably because it's not school holidays yet. My mum has a new boyfriend who likes going fishing, so now *she* likes going fishing, and that's why we're here. What was your name again?"

I make several connections as Carla babbles and poses, my discomfort with her hand-holding rises as I realise her mum and dad aren't together anymore.

"We don't want to be her friend," Rosemary confirms.

The little boy at my feet who I've forgotten about because of Carla's postulating stands up and points at Rosemary.

"Who that?"

I look at the boy in surprise. He's not as small as I thought because he comes up to my chin. I tug my hand away from Carla and step back from the pair of them.

"Wow, even Brody wants to know your name. That is so *rare*, you should be honoured." Carla seems too amazed to notice Brody isn't pointing at me, but at the space beside me.

At Rosemary.

"Who that? Who that?" Brody insists, his gaze flicking between me and Rosemary.

"Tell us your name, Oh Em Gee." Carla rolls her eyes but I barely see her anymore. My heart thuds in my chest as I stare at Rosemary.

What's going on? How can someone else see her too? She's imaginary. She's pretend! The look on Rosemary's face is unreadable, but I can tell she's not happy. Her fists and teeth are clenched and when she turns to look at me, she has the same expression as Mum did with her wide and scary eyes.

"Let's go," she says firmly.

We leave. Before I disappear up the path, I hear Carla's parting comment.

"You're a weirdo!"

I am wading in the lake, wearing my swimmers, shades and a sun hat. The water is refreshingly cold against my skin. Mum lounges on the shore with a paperback in her hand. Every so often she lifts her hand, casting a shadow over her eyes before giving me a flappy wave. I wave back until Rosemary urges me not to. We pretend not to see her and my heart drums in my chest, wondering if I will be called back to shore. When Mum goes back to her reading, I relax and feel a spark of freedom.

"Let's go out farther, it's still shallow," Rosemary suggests. The idea is rebellious and exciting and I head farther out. At first I do it slowly, expecting the sound of my name, but then I am all the way out to my waist without being stopped. When I look back, I am a long way from shore.

"She can still see you," Rosemary says and I nod, but Mum looks like a figurine in a train-set. I see movement and I think she is shielding her eyes, so I wave. She waves back and goes back to her book. I am surprised.

"She can't see *you*, though," I say, feeling brave enough to talk about what happened yesterday. Rosemary says nothing, too busy staring at the ripples on the lake, so I continue. "But he saw you. How?"

Rosemary looks up at me and smiles while

shaking her head.

"He didn't see me, you're remembering it wrong."

I wasn't.

"He wanted to know *your* name. He asked just after Carla did, only with blessedly less words," Rosemary says with a laugh.

He hadn't. He'd asked after Rosemary had spoken. I remember clearly. She looks at me now, expectantly. It strikes me how she doesn't respond to my thoughts and she can see things before I do and then point them out to me. Like rabbits in clouds.

"We should keep going, see how far we get before she calls you back," Rosemary says. Her expression is different today to how it normally is. She has more colour in her cheeks, I can see more of her teeth when she smiles.

"No, I want to stay here."

Rosemary looks frustrated. It is the same look I saw on her face when the boy spoke to her.

"They don't want you," she hisses. I flinch back. "But I do!"

Rosemary lunges for me. Other than widening my eyes, I don't do anything. She grips my head and shoves me into the water. The icy coldness makes me gasp as I go under and my lungs burn. I manage to fight her off and break the surface. Rosemary pushes my head under before I get a good breath but at least I have some air. Her attempts to drown me have me in shock; I can feel the numbness settling over me, sapping my will to fight. I shove her away and try to stand. Waist depth water allows me to stand and splutter for air. I see my sun hat floating away, out of reach, and it renews me into fighting harder. I am coughing more than breathing and Rosemary easily dunks me again.

We are both underwater, her hands on my face, forcing me to look at her. I shouldn't be able to see her clearly in the lake's murk, but I can. She is a vision that captivates me.

"They don't want you, but I do," she repeats softly. "Stay with me forever. Please?"

Her plea wrenches my heart in a way that distracts me from fighting. Maybe drowning will stop hurting if I just breathe the water in and let it take over. Rosemary is right; Mum and Dad want their own lives, separate from each other, separate from me. Each time they fight, I get out of the way and neither of them come after me.

Rosemary has always appeared when I need her. And now she needs me.

Being underwater is like swinging; not part of the ground or part of the sky. Dying is somewhere between rising and falling, a place where I always belonged.

ABOUT THE AUTHORS

Kasper Beaumont

Kasper Beaumont was born and raised in Australia. She combines fantasy and adventure within the *Hunters of Reloria* trilogy; a magical world where halflings and bond-fairies share a quest. www.huntersofreloria.weebly.com

Alicia Bruzzone

Alicia writes for her own amusement, even if no one else finds her funny. Her work has won several short story competitions and has been shortlisted and highly commended enough times for her to feel special.

Linda Conlon

Linda Conlon is a teacher. In her spare time, she co-writes contemporary fantasy novels about world-shifting Wanderers pursued by relentless Authorities. www.WandererOfWorlds.com

Fiona Emily

As well as writing romantic YA, Fiona is a mother of four, a midwife, a singer, songwriter, hopeful dreamer, lover of aromatherapy, long hikes in the wilderness, beautiful scenery and cute fluffy guinea pigs. www.fionaemily.com

Jodie Lane

Jodie combines her love of travel with fascinating stories from the past. Her time travel adventure novel *'The Siege of Masada'* is available at www.jodielane.com or www.facebook.com/authorjodielane

Sophie L. Macdonald
Sophie uses her psychology background to delve into the darker corners of her characters' minds. She is currently working on a magical realism novel.
http://sophielmacdonald.com/

R. A. Purtill
Short stories and flash fiction are my favourite and most successful forms of writing. I am developing a steampunk novel with Christian themes. I facilitate a writing group in the northern suburbs of Brisbane.
www.raelenepurtill.com

Duncan Richardson
Writer of fiction, poetry, haiku, radio drama and educational texts. His recent stories have appeared in "Subtropical Suspense" and "Lighthouses"
www.facebook.com/duncrich.au

Lorraine A. Slim
Lorraine's passion for writing YA came about reading her teenage daughters' books. She enjoys writing punchy short stories and is tackling her first novel.

Delia Strange
Delia writes sci-fi and fantasy. She describes herself as a cynical introvert with an optimistic outlook.
More books and stories at www.deliastrange.com

David Tofts
David's writing style draws on his own contrasting experiences, the fascinating people he's encountered and his survivalist's sense of humour.

www.ingramcontent.com/pod-product-compliance
Lightning Source LLC
Chambersburg PA
CBHW021022120726
47905CB00009B/3135